JOENNA'S AX

A Tale of Bladesend

JOENNA'S AX

A Tale of Bladesend

Elaine Isaak

Joenna's Ax

A portion of this work originally appeared in small press anthology *Clash of Steel: Demons!* as a stand-alone short story, and was reprinted in *Warrior Women*, from Prime Books, 2016.

Formatted by: emtippettsbookdesigns.com

CHAPTER

ONE

The Orcs Come Calling

KILLING A DEMON WAS ALMOST as difficult as being a man Joenna reflected as she jerked free her ax from the corpse. Crouching in its vast shadow, she scanned the battlefield briefly, hoping to spot her captain or the banner of their company. The darting figures of men could be seen between the hulking figures of the demons. There! She saw the crimson banner held aloft, its bearer defended by three soldiers. A demon towered over them, smacking the feeble standard down before it struck the bearer in two.

Joenna cried out, then cursed herself as a group of demons broke off from the mass and sprang to the attack, their tattered leather wings darkening her view as they came on.

Gritting her teeth against the throb of muscles too long

abused, she fended off the first sword. With the backswing, she hacked the leg off the next demon, the huge creatures blocking each other in their eagerness for blood.

Momentum swung her around to face a third, the reek of its breath staggering her as she ducked the poisoned blade. With a sweep of its ragged wings, the demon sprang into the sky. It howled and a chorus of replies answered.

Joenna stumbled back from the waves of sound, both hands flying to cover her ears. The ax-haft she still gripped gave her a nasty knock on the side of her head. "Blue Lady smother me for a fool!"

Across the ruined field, warriors dropped to their knees, hands pressed to their ears. Like her captain, Joenna had stuffed hers with wads of wool, but the sound came on, rattling her teeth and aching her bones, drawing a shock of pain from yesterday's bruises.

"Shut up, shut up," she chanted through clenched teeth. As she swung wildly, she scanned the corpses and stones, searching for her company and hoping they fared better than the poor sots tossed on the points of demons swords. She had been doing this too long now to feel sick any more, or even to feel much sympathy.

Distantly a horn-blast called her back. The demon's weak wings gave out and it dropped heavily, slamming to the earth in her path. The others shifted away, leaving her to face the shrieker. Its knobbed face split into the parody of a grin, the blood-spattered skin more red than brown.

Snarling, Joenna raised her ax and roared. She roared as if she were giving birth and this monster was the bastard who'd got her there.

For a moment, the beast hesitated, its wings partially furled, its dripping jaws gaping, and Joenna charged, swinging the ax for all that she was worth and more. Short and quick, she ducked the demon blade and carved into its belly.

The creature gave a horrid scream—horrid for its humanity, and Joenna gave a prayer of thanksgiving for the wool which cut the sound. Dark viscera spilled out as the demon struggled backward and fell.

"Come on! Joseph, come!" shouted a hurrying figure.

Thank the Lady, it was the captain! Propping the ax on her shoulder, Joenna leapt the thrashing of the demon's tail to join the retreat. Grabbing wounded comrades and stumbling over the dead, the scattered army fled the shrieking demons. They flung themselves over the ridge of stone, a barrage of flaming arrows fending off the demons in pursuit, letting the soldiers burrow into tunnels too small for demons to follow.

Into the cavern where they had their camp, men straggled by twos and threes. Joenna bent over, hands on knees, catching her breath.

Beside her, the captain stopped to clap her on the shoulder. "Good work, Joseph—if we'd a few more like you, we'd rout those bastards, eh?"

Despite her exhaustion, Joenna snorted her laughter. "There aren't no more like me, Gavin. You've got the original." She plucked the wool from her ears and wiggled her jaw to clear out that stuffed-up feeling.

He laughed back, pushing the red shag of hair from his

face, leaving it red with blood. "Aye, well, if more men were inspired. . . " he trailed off, his excitement fading. "Gods, I'm sorry, Joseph. I don't mean. . ."

She straightened and nodded once. "Aye, Gavin, I know. If every man who lost a son joined battle with us today."

He lowered his gaze. In a softer voice, he asked, "Have you made your mark yet?"

Grunting, Joenna lifted the ax once more and stroked the smooth wood of its handle. A dozen years ago, she taught her boy to hew logs with this very ax, the weapon now used to avenge him. The head had none of the fancy work some smiths were prone to, but it kept a good edge and was not so large that a boy, or a woman, would have trouble to wield it. Just below that head, twelve notches chinked the wood. She wiped away the new sheen of blood already turning the notches to the dark, aged brown of the rest of the wood. Slipping a knife from her belt, Joenna hesitated. "Two for sure . . . and a leg wound." Raising an eyebrow at Gavin she offered a smile. "To be honest, the morning's a bit of a blur, isn't it?"

"I saw you take one by the river, early on, then we were hard-pressed for a while. I lost track of you. For a moment I thought—"he broke off. "We're down four men today, that's only six of us from the troop remaining." Again, he scrubbed a hand over his face. More red streaked his ruddy cheeks and trailed down into his beard.

Joenna frowned, then turned back to her ax. "Makes three, then." Carefully, she cut three new notches. Fifteen. Seven more to go to make the total of his years, her son's life cut short in this damnable war. "That your own blood, Cap'n?" The long-ingrained urge to care for his wound prodded at her conscience but four months of playing her role kept her still.

Gavin stared into his hand. "Aye, it may be. I keep wiping it off, but I feel only the dirtier for it." He stiffened, his glance sharpening. "Oh, Gods." He turned abruptly, striding away.

Tracking his gaze, Joenna found a small party approaching. Dressed in the dull camouflage of scouts, they walked stooped over, black hair sticking out in tufts from misshapen heads. Heavy swords that would have reached her breast were strapped across their backs. Her stomach knotted when she saw them, but she merely nodded acknowledgement, seeing the slant of exhaustion in their long limbs.

The leader stopped and blinked at her, then gave a queer grin, wide open to show his snagged teeth. "Don't you run with your captain when the orcs come calling?" His guttural voice grated on her ears, but she stood her ground.

When the orcs come calling. Joenna shuddered and swallowed hard, her eyes dropping for a moment, then she shook her head. "Your mother was no orc, was she?"

"Doesn't matter to your kind, does it?"

Growling, his two companions trotted off, their long arms dangling dangerous fists.

Joenna gave them a sidelong glance, then faced the half-orc before her. "What's your name, then?"

"Are we playing at questions?" He shook back his hair—longer than her own, and more comely since she had hacked hers off without a thought to appearance. The face revealed, once he closed his mouth, looked nearly human. To be sure, his nose was over-large and flat, and his eyes a curious dull black, like two cauldrons freshly scrubbed.

Now that she stood still, the aches returned with full ferocity and Joenna groaned, dropping the ax to put her hands at her back. She was too old for this. "Get on with you—if you can't have a civil conversation, I've done with it."

The half-orc's fingers twitched and his big nostrils flared as if he smelled magic. His eyes narrowed, then widened over another grin. "Valanor, like the hero of old. My mother read the classics." He hissed the last word, drawing it out. His mother was a lady, then, and if he had been another son, he would have been a knight riding with the king's men rather than a scout derided by the very men he served.

Joenna nodded her understanding. "Mine's Joseph. You know a lad named Loref?"

Pulling himself up almost straight and a good deal taller than she, Valanor replied, "Aye. He rode with the ones who went after the dragon—and died there, I'm told."

"He was a friend of mine."

Valanor regarded her, his black eyes unblinking, then he tossed back his head and laughed, the sound raucous and brutal in its bitterness. "Cor—I didn't think you full-bloods could turn your spite so subtle. A friend of yours? What's that make me, your brother?" His cackling broke off and he spat on the ground at her feet. With a snarl low in his throat, he spun away and caught up with his kin in long, loping strides.

"What'd they have to say to you, eh? Nothing good, I'll

warrant," Gavin rumbled returning with a fresh bandage wrapped around his forehead.

Joenna opened her mouth to answer from her anger and exhaustion, then clamped it shut again when the general stomped up. She dropped a short bow, gasping against the confines of the breastplate which held her too tightly. Breastplate—now there was an irony!

"Captain, Joseph." The general nodded to each in turn. "Good work out there."

"Thank you, sir," Gavin replied, then hesitated until the general prompted, "What is it?"

"Had a thought just now, sir." Gavin looked off where the half-orcs had gone, a little enclave surrounding a grubby pond where they set about their compulsive bathing. "Demons don't care for that sort any more than we do, do they?"

The general gave a noncommittal whuff through his graying mustache.

"Well, what if we put them in a vanguard attack, get the demons so bent on ripping them up that we might get an edge on them?"

"You can't do that," Joenna blurted, drawing the officers' keen eyes to her. She floundered, then finally said, "They're our scouts, sir. Without their noses, we'd not know where the demons are."

"True, true," the general snapped, "But we know where the damn things are—"he thrust his arm toward the roof— "they're at our very doorstep!"

"Just so!" cried Gavin, matching the general's fervor.

"And we need a change of tactics. This may be the very thing. Good thinking, Gavin." He gave the captain an approving smile, tight-lipped and regal, then ruffled his mustache, staring toward the scouts and nodding to himself.

Across the room, Valanor hitched a thumb in their direction, gesturing to his comrades as he told his tale, the new joke some full-blood had tried on him. Joenna, despite her age and uniform, felt her cheeks flush. She gritted her teeth, then said, "Sir?"

"Mmm?" A gray eyebrow arched at her.

She took a deep breath. "These half-breeds—they'll need a leader, someone brighter than they are to bring this thing off."

"Mmm." The general frowned, flicking his glance to Gavin, then around the cavern to the other commanders minding the battered remnants of the army.

Joenna, too, looked to Gavin, noting the sudden pallor of his wounded face. "I was thinking, sir, that you'll not like to waste a good officer on this, and I know I'm no officer at all—and not like to be—"she chuckled, hoping to strike a note of humor, and failing, she plunged ahead—"but I'll do it, sir, if that's your will." For her son's sake she stood firm.

"Joseph," Gavin muttered, "it's suicide," but the general focused down his long nose at her, mustaches bristling.

"You raise a point," the general mused. "You do raise a point."

"Please, sir," she glanced toward the scouts. "What better way to avenge my son?"

"Yes, yes." He looked her up and down, frowning at the

top of her head, but nodding at the heft of her ax. "Good lad, your boy. Keep the rabble together, eh, Joseph, and if you win through, there might be a commission in it for you." He slapped her shoulder and she hid her wince. "Meantime," he drawled, "Get some rest—we'll work out the details. Come, Captain."

She bowed again as they drew away, Gavin looking back at her for a moment. The general leaned over to him and whispered, "What's the name of Joseph's son?" as they left earshot.

At last, Joenna dropped to her aching buttocks and loosened the breastplate. Her breasts underneath seemed to protest their freedom almost as much as they had protested the close-quarters. She drew a long, shaky breath and lay back, pillowing her head on her sack of worthless belongings. They'd tell her the plan some time, and probably tell her troops when they kicked them out of bed for the assault— why bother to warn the rabble? Her mouth tasted sour, and the backs of her eyes throbbed to the pulse of her heart. Tomorrow, she would lead the half-orcs in a feint against the demons, hoping to kill her seven, even if she never again notched her ax. Tomorrow, she would die.

CHAPTER

TWO

Joseph's Charge

THE THOUGHT WAS STILL IN her mind the next morning as
Gavin introduced her to the company that she would lead,
with the general looking down his nose at the lot of them.
The half-orcs, awakened early to this news, glared at her from
their kettle-black eyes. They squatted on their haunches,
long arms dangling, long fingers working into fists and back
again as if they sought a throat to close over.

"And if we don't?" said Valanor. "If we refuse to follow
that—"a sharp gesture at Joenna—"to this slaughter in the
making?"

"You shall be ignoring a direct order and I shall have
you slaughtered by your own army. They may be only too
happy to comply. Have I made myself clear?" The general
leaned back on his heels, the three feathers of his golden

helmet bobbing over his shoulders. "I am giving you the unprecedented opportunity to die with an honor you do not deserve, and to see that our forces win out." He pivoted on his heel to give Joenna the benefit of his regard. "This charge, if successful, shall be known as Joseph's Charge, with full credit where it is due. Best of luck. We'll be an hour behind you." He gave a stiff nod and left them.

"You're a brave man, and a good soldier," Gavin murmured close to her ear. "Lady be with you."

Straightening from her bow, Joenna found thirty glaring half-orcs shifting before her. A few glanced toward the archers whose job it was to be sure they followed orders, then back to her, baring their sharp teeth.

"What's it to be, frontal assault? Shall we bother with swords, or will that only make it harder for the demons to shred us?" Valanor loomed over her.

Ducking his gaze, she hefted her ax and propped it on her shoulder. "Blue Lady, There's got to be a way through this," she muttered.

"Yeah," cried a harsh voice, "kill the general!"

The dark mass stilled as the archers drew their bows, searching for the joker. "Who said it?" called a blond sergeant. "Point him out, or we'll open on the lot of you."

"Not if we get you first," snarled one of the crowd, and the half-orcs drew together as the archers advanced. Beyond them, the mass of the army, sharpening swords and checking the buckles on their armor, paused to watch. Even so few half-orcs, with their agility and strength, could make good that threat, tearing into the army until all thirty were dead.

Bowstrings drew taut, arrows nocked, and the soldiers behind stood at the ready as the half-orcs fingered their swords, weighing the odds.

At their head, Valanor kept himself still, addressing his comrades. "Think, would you—it's better to die on the field than in this cave."

The dark group swayed as if they weren't so sure.

A crew pushed through the army, carrying the barrel of rotten meat they used to keep the scouts in line. Its stink preceded them, and the half-orcs recoiled, giving ground before the archers.

"Enough!" Joenna shouted. "Enough, we've got a job to do." She sharpened her glance toward the archer-sergeant, who offered a curt nod, and swung his men away, providing the opening for the company to move forward, out of the cavern. They gulped in the breeze across the caves, the fetid barrel brought behind as an encouragement, then they scrambled up the steep slope toward their death.

Above, the air reeked of fire and blood, and the unmistakable sickly stench of demons not far off. At her back, the half-orcs retched and gasped for breath. She ran her eye over them. Thirty young men, the age of her own boy, marred by the hideous orc features. Their knuckles whitened on their sword-hilts just like any other men. "There's got to be a way."

Close by, Valanor snorted. "Don't fool yourself, full-blood. We face the one army or the other and you get the glory when we're dead—twice as much for volunteering to serve with us." He hissed the syllables like a curse. "As appealing as it sounds, killing the general would only confuse the issue."

"Aye, killing the general. Pity we can't kill theirs."

"You know how they fight, better than we do, I'll warrant. They're like insects, one leader dies and another takes its place with a damnable shriek. They don't wear feathered hats to tell us who's in charge." He tossed his shaggy head, growling low in his throat.

As they started the long trudge up the slope, the archers taking their places, Joenna turned over in her mind the events of the previous day. She had cut down one demon, and another came, leaping up with that shriek. "But they can't all fly," she mumbled to herself.

"They've all got bloody wings, but can't none of them fly more than a few feet straight up."

"Those're the ones that shriek, though," she said, hesitating, looking ahead to the field. Dim dawn's light began to creep over the shapes of the dead. Somewhere across the field, the enemy hunched down, waiting. "The shriekers are the leaders, I think, not just one of them, but any one of them. We kill one, another takes his place and they fight on like nothing's happened."

"You're talking nonsense," Valanor snapped. "And it doesn't matter anyhow to a company of the dead."

But the idea was taking form, and Joenna waved away his despair. "Do they smell different?"

"What?"

"The ones that can fly, do they smell different?"

"They all reek like a week-old murder."

"Come on," she tipped her head toward the battlefield,

then faced her surly crew. "You lot stay a minute, and keep low. Come on," she urged Valanor again.

With a shrug that rolled from one shoulder to the other, he followed, both of them crouching among the rubble as they shifted their way through the corpses and scorched trees. In moments, they came to the site of yesterday's stand, where Joenna had taken down the shrieking demon. "This one," she pointed. "Does it smell different than the others?"

Losing his grin, Valanor glanced down at the wreck of the demon, and his face in the vague light looked pale. A flood of fluids and intestines clogged the path. To her, the thing smelled much the same as a live one, it hadn't had enough time to rot in the short hours they had been sleeping. Catching Valanor's eye, she grimaced. "Sorry. Hard to imagine what it's like for you, with that sensitive nose and all."

His eyes narrowed and he bent down over the demon's head, then over that of her first victim. Immediately, he rose again, turning away, his throat working as if he fought down bile.

She set a hand on his arm. "Sorry, mate. Gods, I am sorry."

Snarling, he shook her away, then leaned in close, taking a sniff of her and baring his teeth. "You're a lying, stinking bastard like the rest of them—woman," he spat.

Joenna jerked back from him, catching her breath.

Valanor advanced and she dare not move again, dare not reveal them before they were ready, as if they ever could be. "Aye, this sack of stink smells different. Rotten, with a hint

14

of evil a little sharper than the rest. Oh, aye, he does, but so do you." He shot out a long finger, the claw scratching her breastplate. "You smell like baby-making and kitchen-cooking and stitching on a pillow. Paugh! Somewhat funny about you I thought yesterday." He tapped his blunt nose with a hooked nail. "Just the sweat, or the blood, or what, but now I see it, you bloody liar. What if I go back in and tell your man? Your Gavin, is he the reason you're here? No, I'll take it to the general—if he'd hear me—"a cackle passed his curled lips. "Maybe that'd give us time to get out of here without all of us losing our necks." He rose away from her, still hunched, and started to turn.

Lunging forward, Joenna caught his arm and yanked him down. Both landed hard on the slimy stones.

Valanor knocked her away, sweeping the sword from his back, his teeth bared as he crouched over her. Joenna flipped up her ax, catching his blade and turning it with the wooden handle, a new and unintended chink appearing through the stain.

Hooking her feet on a stone she yanked herself downward and out from under, ramming aside his sword with the flat of her ax. Despite his strength, the half-orc was a scout, not a soldier, and Joenna allowed herself a slender smile.

With a heave, he flung her off again, propelling himself back toward the line.

Joenna dove, the ax ahead of her, catching his ankle and toppling him even as their archers took aim.

She pushed herself up beside him, proving her conquest to the rearguard as she faced him. "Watch yourself, you bloody bastard!"

His cauldron eyes glinted fire as his lips twisted. "Will I be the next notch on your ax, oh mighty woman? You do your captain proud."

She lowered her weapon, arms shaking with the rush of fighting. Mastering herself, she whispered, "It's not Gavin I'm fighting for it's my son. Don't you see?" She wiped back her hair, matching his fierce expression.

His face, inches from hers, looked more wrong than ever, the heavy single brow furrowing down in his disgust. "Oh, aye, nobility, honor, sacrifice. I know all about that from those accursed stories my mammy tossed aside. I think she died from the shame of it, or maybe from the sight of me, as if it were my fault the orcs took her, my fault what they did to her." His fist rapped against his narrow chest as his hushed voice moved into a low wail of unanswered pain.

Joenna snatched his fist, the hairy strength of it captured by her two small hands. "What they did to me," she said. "To me."

After a moment, Valanor let out a breath through flaring nostrils. He swallowed, his shaking fist twisting in her grasp, but not yet applying his strength to freedom.

"Aye, they came to my house, too. I never seen a brute so awful, not until this war. That raiding party, they broke and beat and took what they would." She gave a short, nasty laugh. "Look at me, Valanor. I make a better man than a woman—I'm so ugly, no man would take me to wife. But I was good enough for orc-bedding, wasn't I? My parents cast me out. Most families did, I hear. And there I was with child—

this gangly, awful, screaming little baby." Dropping his hand, she scrubbed tears from her face, shaking her head to clear them. "And I thought. . . two things as ugly as us, we might as well love each other."

Her chin rapped against her breastplate as she wept, her ragged hair flopping around her face. Cursing herself, she fought the tears, drawing long breaths, snorting like an ass.

Nearby, Valanor breathed in little gasps. After a long time, he said, "Loref. He was your son."

"Aye."

"He's the reason you fight, the reason you've got those notches in your ax."

More calmly, the tears trickling away at last. "Aye."

"He is. . . he was, like me." His voice became a hot breath across her damp face.

Joenna faced him fully. "Aye," she said. "Like you."

They sat beneath the growing light, surrounded by demon filth and demon stench and Valanor stared at her from his dull-black eyes, so like her son's. Finally, he glanced back to the shadows that concealed his kin. "You've got a plan, haven't you? You've thought of something."

"It won't save us, I don't think, but it may cause confusion enough that the others can win. Valanor—"she took a deep breath and expelled it, along with the grief she could not afford—"it may be enough to show those bastards you're not to be spat on."

A grin started at the corner of his thin lips. "I doubt it."

After a sigh, she said, "I doubt it, too, but at least we'll know we did our best. Will you help me? We'll have to convince the company."

"That we will." He rose into a crouch, then cocked his head at her. "What's your name, Loref's mother?"

"Joenna."

"So, Joenna's Charge."

"Naw." She touched the head of her ax. "Better to call it, Half-orc's Revenge."

The troop had few complaints—any plan was better than what they'd been ordered—and they fanned out around Joenna and Valanor. Quickly, closely, they began their advance. They rippled over the stones and bodies like a shadow not yet dispelled by the feeble light of day. It felt like miles, jogging over the rough ground when the demons rose up, shrieking before them.

The vile wind of their voices slapped back the attackers, but the troop shifted and swirled around her. Instead of attacking, Valanor and Joenna threw themselves under the first swords. They dodged and sprinted and Valanor sniffed the air. Wherever he pointed, there they struck.

The company plunged in with them, knocking aside the demons as best they could, crying out to block the sound of demons shrieking. One demon leapt up, flapping, over and over, its voice howling out the commands. Three of hers went down in the first strike and Joenna set her jaw against the dread.

Rather than driving straight on, Joenna's force moved as if at random, following the whims of Valanor's nose. The shrieking filled her ears and echoed inside her aching skull.

Grimly she followed where the half-orc lead.

Joenna's ax defended him, cleaving the arm from this demon, slicing into the leg of that one, until he could finger a shrieker and they set-to and brought it down.

The half-orcs swirled around them, slaying the marked ones, themselves falling beneath the poison blades, this one hacked in two, that one crushed by taloned arms. The gray of the scouts vanished beneath a wash of red. The distant sound of horns announced the army's coming—if any of hers would be left alive to see.

A great demon sprang up before them, outspread wings heaving to get it off the ground as it shrieked.

A lash of its tail caught Joenna broadside and she tumbled over the ground, sprawling with her ax underneath. "Blue Lady," she cried, as the demon thudded to the ground again, one ragged wing scraping along her legs.

The demon leapt away, a wail of pain escaping it. Demon blood spattered Joenna's face as she rolled and snatched up her ax.

Bellowing, it snatched toward Valanor, slapping aside his sword at the cost of its own fingers. It lunged again, the half-orc scrambling across the ground.

Matching its bellow, Joenna buried her ax in the demon's side.

She slammed to earth as it spun around, and its sword bit into her shoulder.

The demon's head filled her vision, its fangs dripping as it gaped over its prize. The head reared back for another shriek and dove toward her, gaping.

With her off-hand, Joenna whipped free her knife and rammed it home into a smoldering eye.

Blood spurted, obscuring her vision, then the breath whoofed from her lungs as the demon collapsed on top of her.

For a long time, the world went silent. Joenna thanked the Lady for this reprieve, promising to visit Her temples the first chance she got. If there ever were a chance. In the meantime, she struggled to drag air into her lungs past the steaming corpse that covered her.

Thunk! Thunk! The sound penetrated her fog, and Joenna cracked open her eyes, shaking her head to clear them. Thunk! The steady sound of an ax into wood. "Loref?" she croaked.

The weight bearing down on her fell aside and he stood over her, ax in hand, shoving the severed demon from her chest.

Letting the ax-head rest beside hers, Valanor bent down, his eyes skimming her face and form. Agile, hairy fingers stroked the blood from her eyes. "Praise the Gods, you're alive!"

"You, too," she managed, sucking in great breaths and coughing them back out again. "Like to smothered me, that beast." She moved as if she could rise, but Valanor held her back, plucking the wool from her ears.

"Listen!" He shouted.

"Can't hear a damn thing." Joenna slapped her ear with her right hand. The left one only twitched numbly.

"No shrieking! They're in retreat from us, a bunch of

accursed half-breeds, before the damned army even got here!" His laughter sparkled with sudden hope, echoing the horns which drew the army past. Valanor leaned in closer. "You're wounded. Joenna, I'll get you to the surgeons." He bent to gather her up.

Snatching his hand she rattled. "Don't. They'll know."

He glanced to her stained breastplate and gave a brief nod. "Aye. They'll send you home to get over all this, you fool woman."

She shook her head. "How many?" she asked.

"How many what?"

"Demons I killed."

Looking at the sky, Valanor considered, then settled his black gaze back on her face. "Five."

"Then I'm not through yet." She shoved herself into a sitting position, his arm hovering near her. "Don't haul me from here like a fragile woman. If you want to be useful, raise me up like a man."

"But you're wounded! Surely this battle is honor enough."

Shaking her head again, Joenna told him, "I've two more notches to carve, my friend." Then she grinned up at him. "Valanor, hand me my ax."

CHAPTER

—∞—

THREE

Forging the Blade

WITH VALANOR'S HELP, JOENNA ROSE to unsteady feet. It was true: the demons shrieked now only with pain and confusion, as the cheering human army drove them from the field. The pair stood watching for a moment, as the battle moved on without them, then Joenna looked for her own men. Two crouched not far off, assisting a third, evidently wounded. A few more hovered in the middle distance, looking to the army, then back toward the caves they had left.

Joenna raised her good right arm and stuck two fingers in her mouth, emitting the sharp whistle she used to use to rouse her sheepdog.

The half-orcs froze and turned, and she waved them back. They were better saved for their skills than spent in mopping up the retreating demons. Loping and limping, the remnant of her company gathered round. Two needed help, and of the other fifteen, most bled from gashes to arms and backs for they had no armor. If they were to go on fighting like this, Joenna would see that that was changed.

At last, the company assembled, complete, and down by more than a third. They watched her warily, flicking dark glances to the one of their number who supported her.

"It worked," blurted a latecomer, lapsing into a grin that earned him a few glares from the others, but an equal number of answering smiles.

"It did," she said, "and you're all responsible. No matter what happens next, you remember that this was your victory—that lot—"she waved toward the rest of the army— "hid in a cave while we got it done."

"Our victory?" said one of them, a stocky fellow, for an orc. "Don't you mean your victory, Joseph's Charge, eh? You're the one who'll get the commission out of it, and the honor."

"Don't try your luck, Koresh—we're only alive because of Joseph's plan," Valanor put in.

"Which only worked because of your nose." Koresh tapped his own.

"Aye," said Joenna, raising her voice despite the sharp pain at her shoulder. It settled in with an awful heat, as if the blade still burned inside her. "Aye, it's true, and all your swords, and I'll not deny it no matter who's asking. I say again that this is your victory, not only that, but you all know how to tell the shriekers now, am I right? They'll be needing you more than ever before to finish off this war, and that can't be a bad thing."

"They'll make it one," Koresh spat back. "Somehow, they will." Then he tossed back his head with a nasty laugh. "What'm I saying? You will—you're one of them, after all."

Joenna let her chin drop against her breastplate and sighed. Her mind felt numb, and growing number. Beside her, Valanor stretched to his full height. "You don't know what you're talking about, Koresh. You remember Loref, right? The best of us, we all said so—"he broke off as Joenna let her ax drop, whacking his foot, and he stared at her sharply.

"Let'em think what they will," she mumbled. "I need," a gasp of pain, "I need—"

"Aye, you do," he snapped, with a nod to acknowledge what she did not say: that she needed her secrets kept, and he would keep them. "Surgeons."

"Sir," called a fainter voice, and she found a half-orc before her, his sword held down in both hands, "we don't all think like him."

She mustered a grin, but it felt shallow. "I'm glad of it. What's your name, then? And the rest of you, too—I think we best get to know each other."

"Brion," he answered, and gave the duck of his head that served for a bow. The nature of their parentage left the half-orcs a motley bunch, some, like Valanor seemed more human, comfortable with the hunched posture most used, but also capable of standing straight as men—the better to take advantage of their height and long reach. Others, like Brion, walked with a perpetual stoop, their upper spines curved so that their knuckles brushed the grass. It made them look like their orc-ish fathers, and gave the full-bloods more reason to revile them.

The company formed a ragged roll-call, given names only, since most were denied the right to their family names. "Dale. . . Rogan . . . Marcus . . . Lassiter. . . Joram. . . Iren. . . Callifrax—"another classical name, Joenna registered—"Shane. . . Orris. . . Therren. . . Janev. . . Norven. . . Garret. . .Karrel. . . Havnor." Most of them met her eye as they spoke, with challenge or simply curiosity.

Joenna returned the slight bow. "Let's go back and rest up; I reckon there'll be more for us to do before too long."

Four of them grouped around to carry Havnor, his head wound spilling a trail of blood on the slow march back to the caves. The archers on the ridge hesitated, their bows still nocked, and, failing any orders to the contrary, let them pass despite the continued fighting the company left behind. Joenna took the lead, walking carefully, cradling her left elbow, until she stumbled on the steep slope, slithering several feet and losing her ax.

Without a word, Valanor gathered the ax and stuck it through his belt before he lifted her back to her feet and brought her in with him, crying "Surgeons! We've got wounded."

The surgeons—a small enclave tending yesterday's casualties—glanced over, then murmured amongst themselves before one of them went down the tunnel toward the general's private nook.

Taking most of her weight, Valanor brought her to a pile

of rubble used as a bench and let her down. Sitting on the cave floor, he loosened her breastplate, pushed back the cut sleeve and examined the wound. At last, he leaned back with a low rumble.

"What?" she demanded.

"It's deep, and a bad angle." He met her gaze, then shifted his glance away toward the others, straggling in and settling around their pool, beginning to tend each other's wounds.

"What," she said again, the growing weariness drooping her eyelids.

Valanor's eyes returned to her face, his broad mouth showing a grimace. "The wound's burning isn't it?" he muttered, looking back to the half-orcs again.

"Like a bonfire," she agreed.

Nodding, he gave a sound which might have been a sigh. "We're proof against the poison," he told her. "The full-bloods aren't supposed to know—we figured it out in training—not that they listen to us much, anyhow, but we realize what would happen if we told." He shrugged, the motion rolling from one shoulder to the other.

Joenna frowned, then drew back a moment. "Aye—you'd be in the vanguard every time."

"And there'd be none of us left by now. Thing of it is, if I clean your wound, it won't burn so much." He glanced toward the surgeons, but they showed no sign of stirring on behalf of orc-bloods. "It takes blood," he said, "or spit."

Joenna tried to bring her arm into view, and winced with the effort as a spasm of pain followed by fire shot toward her chest. "Do it," she said, "anything that helps."

"Right." Valanor took a hold of her arm and wiped away the blood, then spat into the gash, several times.

Flinching, Joenna shut her eyes, and wondered for a moment why she trusted him, for all that he reminded her of her son, then she gave a long sigh as the burn in her flesh died back to a dull throb. She popped her eyes open and stared again at the cut, then up at Valanor and grinned. "It works."

"It's our secret, right?"

Across the room, the human wounded moaned and sobbed, and Joenna hesitated.

"Right?" he repeated, his voice sharp.

"Aye," she said at length. "Pity we can't help them, tho." She chuckled suddenly. "Maybe we could bottle it, eh?"

Ruffling back his scruffy hair, Valanor shook his head. "You're full of ideas today."

"Hey, the last one was—"

"Take him!" someone shouted.

Four soldiers of the general's guard pounced on Valanor, knocking him to the floor and flinging away his sword.

"Great Gods," Joenna cried, "Let him up! What're you doing?"

One of the surgeons pointed. "He spit on Joseph, while he was cleaning the wound. I saw it."

"Well, if he—"Joenna broke off, jaw hanging limp as they hauled Valanor to his knees. He stared at her, black eyes anxious, and inclined his head toward the other half-orcs with a little shake. Secrets. She clamped her jaw, dropping her aching head to her hand. He kept her secret, now she must keep his, even at the cost of whatever punishment they wrought.

Accompanied by another surgeon, the general stepped up, his mustache freshly trimmed, and gave a sharp nod. "You did well, Joseph. I'll make you a sergeant, and these men will tend you while you get some rest. Meantime, we'll take care of this one." He narrowed his eyes at Valanor.

"Thank you, sir, I mean, no, sir—it's not necessary. Just having his joke, I'm sure," Joenna stammered.

"To spit on a soldier, never mind on his own officer, is a disgrace and an insult we cannot countenance."

"But after the way they fought and all, sir, don't you think—"

Shaking his head so that the feathers on his helmet tossed to and fro, the general said, "'Twas only your leadership that forged this bunch into a weapon today—we can't afford for them to get above themselves. Archer told me he saw you brawling with that one on the field, right off; I suspect he's got some grudge against you, Joseph, and we can't have it. Bring the barrel."

As his men turned to obey, Valanor stiffened, the dark hair a sharp contrast to his sudden pallor. "No, sir, I meant no insult, I only thought—"

"I've not asked you to speak, have I?" The gray brows notched upward, inviting a reply, but Valanor froze, his mouth gaping around his queer teeth, and Joenna held her breath until he shut it, and turned his face away. His long arms trembled in the soldiers' grip as the barrel scraped into view.

Weak and weary, Joenna felt her gorge rise at the scent of it, and she reeled. The surgeons caught her, propping her up as they worked over her wound. Around the pool where the half-orcs bathed, they crouched or lay like statues, their ugly faces arrested by the scene unfolding. One of them—Brion, it looked like—shuffled a little closer, kneeling down to listen, hands on his knees.

Her throat working to keep back the sickness, Joenna watched with reluctant eyes as they shoved the barrel to a level place.

Clutched by four men, Valanor strained back. "No, please, sir, no, I spent the morning smelling demons dying. I can't stand this, sir—beat me, flog me, do what you will, but I can't take the barrel, not now."

His quiet pleading, so unlike the brash manner she was used to, shook Joenna to the core, for Loref's voice echoed in her skull and it was all she could do not to weep. She slapped away the surgeon's hand and pushed herself up. "Sir, there's got to be some other punishment."

They dragged Valanor closer, and the general shook his head. "Not thinking clearly, eh, Joseph?" He chuckled. "Well, you did admit to not being officer material. No, the very fact that he protests it means that this is the only fit punishment: the only thing likely to break him to proper discipline. We'll get you trained up yourself, you'll make out well, I think." He nodded his satisfaction, and motioned for the soldiers to carry on.

Putting their full effort into it, they hauled the half-orc to the barrel, wrapping his arms around it, his face up against the wood. Dark, foul liquid seeped down the side. "I'm sorry," he cried, "please don't—please!"

Someone shook Joenna gently, and pushed her back down, "Come on, Joseph, you've got to relax your arm if we're to do any good."

"Give him an extra hour for every word he speaks from here out," the general ordered, "including those last five."

Joenna's stomach knotted. They shoved Valanor up to the barrel, on his knees to embrace the thing, his wrists snapped into manacles attached at the back. In her four months with the army, she had seen the barrel applied two or three times—not to Valanor, but perhaps Koresh, she realized now. It stunned her each time, these powerful, brutish people reduced to begging: the threat alone normally held them in check. Each time, she prayed to the Blue Lady that they had never done it to Loref. Even among half-bloods, he had a keen nose; but no, he'd been raised obedient and happy, and quiet like herself, not the sort to get in trouble and require such a punishment.

Tucking his head to his shoulder, Valanor gasped for breath. His throat worked savagely, and his body shook all over. His forehead knocked against the wood and he vomited down his chest, sobbing and retching until it seemed he might choke on the absence.

Joenna's throat felt raw, and she realized that she was snarling, deep and low, with a fury she could voice no other way. The skin at her shoulder pinched and twitched as the surgeon stitched her back together, murmuring soothing noises as if her anger were directed at him. Her clenched fists lay in her lap, but her right hand shook with the desire to take up her ax, lying side by side with Valanor's sword, and hack through the bonds. The stench encouraged the soldiers to retreat several paces, their faces wrapped with kerchiefs soaked in some perfume.

"So," the general said, puffing out his mustache, and smoothing it down again with two fingers, "he'll recover, then? Good, I'd like to deploy the scouts with the third regiment, across the plain. Mayhap we can get this cleared up before the king arrives; his majesty will appreciate our efforts. Rest up, I'll arrange everything."

He added a flick of his clean hand to dismiss her into medical care, and Joenna, held by the surgeon's patient hands, gave thanks that she need not salute him. Her jaw creaked, and she urged herself to relax, then called out, "How long'll you leave him there?"

One of the soldiers, glowering down at Valanor's wretched bound body, said, "'til dawn, I guess—boosts morale for the rest of the troops when they get back, eh?"

"No doubt," she growled, noticing the sweat that dampened his brow and the strain in his shoulders. He trembled like a child, like her own Loref caught in a nightmare, and she had no power to wake him. Or had she? She scanned the cave, ducking the stares of her own company.

"Come along, Joseph," the surgeon said, drawing her up, "Let's get out of the stink."

"I'd like to get my things, if you don't mind. Just over there." She pointed her chin toward the little bundle forsaken on the ground.

"I'll get it," said the other, and set off while they limped toward the makeshift infirmary. They settled her to one side, with a few others not too badly off, and she took a few deep breaths, clearing the scent of the barrel from her lungs, avoiding the sight of it. The surgeon dropped her pack beside her, and returned again in a moment with a steaming mug. "Drink this, it'll help."

"Put me to sleep?" she asked, admitting how nice that sounded about now.

"Aye, it will—you'll need your strength if you're heading out again tomorrow." He pressed it on her, and would not go until she had swallowed it down. She sat a while longer, ignoring the querulous voices of those around her, seeking to know about the battle, then finally gave in to the weakness that suffused her muscles. Valanor would be chained there all night, and the guards would keep their surly watch at least until supper. And it would feel so good to lie down.

She woke with a start in darkness, a few flickering fires lighting up the different companies returned from the mopping up of demons. The half-orcs clustered together on the far side of their pool. Some snored like thunder, rolling in waves across the cavern to the eternal frustration of the full-bloods. Seemed to her that the officers complained a good bit, while the common foot soldiers just got about their sleep as best they could. Her entire arm throbbed, her fingers pulsing with every beat of her heart, but Valanor's spit had worked its charm, for she hadn't lain awake moaning like so many others. Now, to return the favor.

Joenna sat up carefully, and found the pack beside her.

She pulled it into her lap and rummaged through until she seized on what she wanted and drew it out. She did not need light to be sure, but lifted it to her face and gave it a gentle squeeze. The small pillow puffed a scent of lavender and roses, cultivated in their own difficult garden—the only luxuries, and only for her son. She squeezed again and inhaled deeply, the scent growing stronger as her tears wet the herbs and stuffing. Drawing up her knees, Joenna let herself weep for a little while, indulging the tears she could not afford by day, her face buried in this remembrance. Finally, she wiped her face, scrubbing the tears into her weathered skin, and dug around in the bag a little more, finding the length of linen she used as a towel.

Rolling to her knees, Joenna rose, examining the cavern to see who was still wakeful—very few, after the hard day's labor—and set out. As she had suspected, the four guards at the barrel had shifted off to the side with their dice and a jug, and now snored in competition with the half-orcs across the way. It was Loref taught her that the best way to sneak was to seem as if you weren't, and just go for what you wanted with the kind of purpose that convinced the on-lookers you needn't be watched. Smart lad, her Loref. So she sauntered across the cave as if she were expected, then squatted down beside Valanor. The stench assailed her, her stomach heaving, and she had cause to be thankful she hadn't eaten all day.

He shivered and started at her touch. Firelight glinted from his too-glossy eyes, then they became slits of blackness.

Seeing the change, Joenna hesitated, then set her jaw and pulled the towel from the crook of her numb left arm and started to wipe his face with quick movements.

Valanor pulled back, as much as he was able. "Leave me alone," he muttered, his voice hoarse with the damage to his throat. "You're acting like somebody's mother."

Flinching, Joenna balled up the towel. "I was somebody's mother," she hissed in return. "And how would you know how a mother should act—yours never did." Her touch a little more harsh, she finished cleaning his face, and he submitted with that angry glint to his eyes. She lowered the towel, taking shallow breaths through her mouth and feeling smothered even then. "Gods."

The eyes shut, and he whispered, "Aye."

Slipping her hand to her belt, she fingered the little pillow, covered and re-covered in the scraps of fine cloth from the stitchery she used to take in for a few extra coins. In the darkness, she could not make out much of Valanor but the shape of his bent head, tufts of unruly hair thrusting up, unmanageable as her son's had been. She reached out to touch him, then her fingers clenched back into a fist and she took back her hand, lowering her head. "Damn," she breathed, the noxious fumes filling her lungs as she struggled to master herself. She was no mother, not here; she was a soldier named Joseph, leader of a successful charge, sergeant for a crew of half-breeds, wounded in the line of duty and expected to do it all again on the morrow.

"Have you come clean," Valanor rasped, "or is the perfume just for me?"

She opened her hand, the little pillow resting on her palm. "Why'd you have to be so all-fired difficult? Blue Lady."

"Must have been my upbringing."

"Aye." Lifting the pillow, Joenna spoke quick and low, her face warm. "Look, I've got this thing, something I made for my son, filled with sweet stuff, for when we went into town and the smells got to him, you know?" Stupid: of course he knew. "D'you want it?"

To her surprise, Valanor laughed, little more than a few light breaths in the darkness, and his eyes flashed open. "My sergeant brought me a sachet."

The flush deepened, then Joenna laughed in return, and answered, "My soldier spit in my wound, and I forgot to thank him."

"It worked?"

She crushed the pillow in her palm, releasing a drift of scent. "This does, too, after its fashion."

He stayed silent, and, after a moment, Joenna reached out again. She lifted her left hand, grimacing as she forced the action, and cupped his cheek away from the wood, sliding the pillow in beside his face. His skin was smooth—smoother than her own by some length, and she wondered if it might be due to his mother's influence, that unknown lady who birthed and abandoned him. She slipped the pillow in beside his face, and brought her hands away, his cheek resting against a cloud of lavender and roses.

Eyes still shut, Valanor took a shuddering breath, and another, a little deeper. "Go away," he exhaled.

Joenna held to her left arm as she rose. "You're welcome." She lurched back to her place in the infirmary and needed no sleeping draught to collapse into slumber.

CHAPTER

FOUR

H'ors Heritage

SHE WOKE AROUND DAWN, TO the scent of sausages, something she'd not smelled in weeks, as they most often had only the dried meat they'd packed in supplemented by hard biscuits the cooks produced from stored ingredients. Her arm throbbed as she sat up, groaning and clutching her elbow.

"It'd help if you didn't sleep in your armor, Joseph," Gavin said, with a grin. He thrust out a wooden bowl with a pair of steaming sausages.

Joenna accepted it gladly, with a grin of her own. "Glad t'see you made it through," she said around a mouthful—she hadn't eaten a thing since yesterday breakfast.

"Aye, and you—that was more the surprise. We had a bit of a job cleaning up the rest, but the field's ours at last, thanks to your attack. Once you've eaten, the general's got wagons to haul you to the next battle, along with that lot." He lost his grin as he tilted his head toward the half-orcs' enclave.

His attitude, more than his words, jogged her mind, and she overcame the needs of hunger to rise stiffly and turn. At the center of the cavern, the barrel stood, with its sorry prisoner. The guards nearby conferred together, and Joenna was about to go down and tell them to get a move on, the sun was up and her man still in chains, but they finally bestirred themselves. One of them brought out the key and made a little parade around the barrel, swinging it as if he'd forgotten what it was for. Those nearby chuckled a little, but Valanor made no response, even when the guard lifted the key as if to drop it into the barrel's foul contents.

Dropping her sausage, Joenna shoved the bowl back to Gavin and marched across the uneven floor. Her greasy fingers felt cold and shaky as she reminded herself to breathe.

Seeing her approach, the guard stiffened, then squatted down to set the key to the lock, with a roll of his eyes to his companions. They strapped on their protective masks of scent to haul the barrel out by the entrance.

His prop removed, Valanor slowly drew back his arms to cross over his chest, his head still bowed. He twitched once, grunted, and dragged his head up, his chest shaken by ragged breaths. Getting one foot under him, Valanor lurched upright, swayed, and stumbled a few steps forward.

Joenna quickened her pace even as he swayed again, then tumbled headlong across the stone. "Curse them for demon whores," Joenna hissed under her breath.

Around her, the soldiers laughed and hooted, some throwing scraps of food, or blood-stained rags. A few half-orcs rose, and two—Brion and Dale, she thought--bounded forward to Valanor's side. Just as Joenna arrived, they raised him up and brought him, his feet dragging, quickly to their pond. Brion gathered him close and they plunged into the pool, splashing water over Valanor, stripping off his stained shirt. They worked in silence, as if oblivious to the raucous soldiers around them. Koresh stood on a low rise, staring down with narrowed eyes, his teeth glinting between parted lips, but he, too, made no sound.

Joenna stood where he had fallen, mumbling a little prayer of thanks that her fears proved unfounded. Clearly weak from his ordeal, Valanor was strong yet, and he would survive. She found the little sachet and tucked it inside a sleeve. Casting about for a moment, she walked to the mound where they had stopped together the day before. Her left arm held tight to her side, she bent and lifted her ax, thrusting it through its belt-loop, then bent again and heaved up Valanor's enormous sword. It took both hands to lug the thing along with her, but she gritted her teeth and did it, walking up to where Koresh, teeth still bared, awaited.

He thrust out one large, hairy hand and snatched the sword from her grip. "Happy, are you?"

"Are you?" she snapped back. "You two don't seem the best of friends."

"Maybe not, but he's still one of my own, even if he's a daRives, and I'm a charwoman's spawn."

Joenna staggered, or thought she did, and her mouth

flapped stupidly for a moment. "He's what?"

"A daRives, didn't he tell you, Sergeant? Oh, but we're not allowed to tell." He covered his mouth, but could not conceal the pointed grin. Dark eyes flashed up to sweep the room, and his grin grew a little wider.

DaRives. By the Gods and their Mounts—that name made Valanor a cousin to the king. "I don't believe it."

"What, don't he look like royalty?" Koresh swiveled his head, drawing her gaze along with his. Valanor lay with his head pillowed on his arms, the rest of him vanishing into the murky water. Brion crouched nearby, rummaging through a pile until he produced a shirt of the same tough, gray material they all wore. He murmured something, and Valanor's eyes opened, dull and directionless. He blinked at her, then turned away, his shoulders still shaking as he breathed. "Don't he?" Koresh repeated with a snort of laughter.

The funny thing was, Joenna reflected, that he did. From the first, she had found him more comely than most of the others—her own Loref included--his blunt features more refined, his speech distinct and educated. "Cor," she breathed.

"Aye. If he were a man, he'd out-rank you, by a large bite." He snapped his teeth together, then flicked his head toward the far end of the cavern. "The general, too. Instead, he's just another H'or." Koresh used the contraction many full-bloods did, curving his lips around it like a blessing, rather than a curse.

"Aye," she said, "well." She traveled her gaze over the rest of her company, then raised her voice and cleared her throat. "We're to do it all over tomorrow or the next day, down the other front. There may be a few more battles in it for us, before we get to go home." She tried a smile of encouragement, but the half-orcs shared glances that excluded her, and she let it go. "So. Get yourselves ready, get a good breakfast—I don't know where we'll be stopping, eh?" Her gaze settled on Havnor, lying still, his eyes shut, and she picked her way over, ducking Koresh's glare, to squat down.

She knew by the set of his face that he was dead, and she shut her eyes. "Damn."

"One less to kill at the next fight," muttered the nearest half-orc, a fellow with paler hair, nearly brown.

Joenna rounded on him. "Rogan, is it? What I'd like is for all of us to live, you got that?"

"Yes, Sir," Rogan replied, dropping his gaze, his arms crossed, leaving sharp elbows with fingers hanging like a scarecrow's branches.

"Let's get him to the gravediggers."

At that, Rogan shot up, catching her arm before she could turn. "No," he said, an urgent whisper, eyes darting.

His strong hand held her, but Joenna did not test the strength, nor appear to struggle for the distant eyes that must be watching. "Why?"

Rogan ducked his head, and murmured, "Just, please, no. We're leaving, eh? We leave him here, right, Sergeant? Just—"he broke off, the words failing him as his brow furrowed.

"Just trust you," she finished for him. They stood a moment longer, and Rogan released her arm, his fists clenching even as he edged away, preparing for her denial. Joenna looked him over, and gave a one-shouldered shrug—

all that she could manage. "Right. I trust you. Some point, you trust me, and tell me what it's about, eh?"

Flashing a smile that might have frightened a different woman, Rogan said, "Aye, yes, I'll do it."

"Fair enough." She turned away and walked back, black eyes following her movements. At the pool, she again knelt down, fist on her hip, examining Valanor. He breathed now as if in sleep, his narrow chest rising and falling as he lay, his face turned away from her. She looked up and found Brion, his tall frame bent up to almost her own height as he tended his friend. "You take good care of him, right? He's taken good care of me."

Silent, Brion bobbed his head, and Joenna rose, her eyes lingering, before she turned away.

She found Gavin about where she'd left him, and they shared breakfast while he regaled her with the blows he had taken, and those he gave in return. She grunted and listened, and laughed in the right places, and realized that he'd be going home soon, his commission through after yesterday's rout while she and her company went on, until the last of the demons scattered back to wherever they came from. The sausages stayed as a hard lump in her stomach as she gathered her things, and bid her farewells.

Under guard of the archers, her half-orcs clambered up into two farm wagons, Valanor being helped in, and promptly folding into a ball in the corner.

Joenna, aware that it was supposed to be an honor, stood with the general and a few other officers to supervise. Stiffly, she set her feet and watched, ignoring much of the flow of dialog around her, which focused on how glad they were to be rid of the H'or, and speculations on how many would survive. If she spoke, she'd only get angry, so she directed the anger to keeping still, keeping her left arm under control. The caverns they had sheltered in faced a narrow road with a steep drop-off to the other side. The ridge grew ever more rocky toward the mountains far away to the right, but it gentled down into farm land to the left, the distant green patches marked with burned houses and ruined crops from the long war. Her own little patch, Joenna knew, had long since gone the same way. She herself had let it go, when Loref died.

"Sir?" said a guard, with a brief bow.

"What, what?" the general inquired, smoothing his mustache.

"What should be done with that, sir? We'll have no use for it." He pointed, and they followed the gesture. Not far off, the barrel hulked in daylight, black and oozing, its odor swept in curls around them, then away with the humors of the breeze.

"Might load it in, might be needed," the general mused.

With a sharp noise, Joenna drew their eyes, and hoped she sounded dispassionate as she said, "Well, there's not much room as it is, Sir. And I'll wager the other regiments have their own, eh?"

"Right you are. Good thinking, Joseph. Go on and mount up."

Joenna bowed, dismissed, and scrambled up into the second wagon, her short legs dangling over the back.

With a click of his heels, the general turned back to his guard. "Dump it out—no need, as you say."

Bowing smartly, the guard re-grouped his companions to thrust staves through the barrel rings and haul it to the edge of the ravine. As they heaved to tip the huge stink-pot, the bottom panel groaned, then split, sending a rush of foul liquid in both directions. Slender shapes and lumps gushed out with the mess and the guards leapt back, cursing and gagging. One lump rode its flood toward the officers, who sprang back likewise as it came to a stop before them, resting against a rock.

As the wagon lumbered to a start, Joenna stared down from her vantage at the swollen face revealed on the sodden mass—a wide mouth gaping from mushy lips, broad nose eaten out by maggots, wide-set vacant eye sockets. A few tufts of black hair still stuck up from the rotten scalp.

Her guts churned and Joenna clamped a hand over her mouth, bending double to block the sight of the half-orc dead. Four, maybe five such lumps had gone over in the sludge of corpses. Blue Lady—no wonder Rogan refused to tell anyone his friend lay dead. The image flashed before her shut eyes: Valanor embracing the barrel, through the long, dark night—with the butchered remains of his kin inside.

Joenna lost her sausages on the road, and only thanked the Lady that they'd gone far enough Gavin and the general couldn't have seen her. Keeping her shoulders brutally rigid, she stayed in a hunch as the wagon lurched along.

She had never seen the body. The army hadn't wanted to tell her where and how her son had died; the keep went up in flames, they said, there was nothing to see. She knew he'd gone with a knight and his squire, a guide for them on this mission of their own seeking, the mission that started the end of the war. She knew that much only because the army came looking for Loref, to see if he had really died, or if he had deserted and run home.

In her hidden, smothered lap, Joenna knotted her hands together. "Blue Lady, tell me my son's gone with you. Tell me he's not rotting in a barrel some terrible place, oh, please," she murmured, though she knew there could be no response.

The sun beat down on her back before she mastered her emotions and turned, drawing her legs up into the wagon. To both sides, the half-orcs slumped against the slats, some asleep, some talking in low voices, two or three eying her. Meeting their eyes, nodding, she made her way to the far corner, where Valanor lay, and propped herself against the back of the carter's seat.

As the wagon rattled over the rough road, Valanor stirred and opened one eye at her. Sighing, he pushed himself up and draped against the slats.

For a time, they regarded each other that way, expressionless, jogged back and forth by the motion of the wagon. Finally Valanor shifted position, crossing his wrists on top of one knee and said, "How's the arm?"

"Not bad."

He cracked a grin. "You can barely move it. Will you be up to this battle?"

"Naw. But I'll do it anyhow. How about you?"

The grin dwindled. "I'm fine—very resilient, we H'ors."

44

"Don't say that," she protested, glowering, "besides—" she shut her mouth, trying not to give in to her curiosity, but he had already followed her there.

"Koresh's been talking again, about things he shouldn't."

"Is it true?"

Valanor's eyes narrowed, and he leaned forward, his sharp shoulders drawn up like some great vulture. "You want the whole story? I'll tell you, if you answer one question for me."

His sudden intensity put her off a little, but Joenna shrugged. "Go on—you already know my secrets."

His glance flickered over the sleeping forms nearest before he spoke again, in a whisper, "You claim to be this loving mother—how could you sign away his life?"

"I don't know what you mean."

With a snarl of laughter, he said, "No? They came to your house, knocked on the door and hauled your son away, and you don't know what I mean?"

"I recall all that, of course I do." She, too, glanced at the others, insuring their privacy. "Man gets called up to the army, he goes—Loref wasn't afraid."

Some of the hostility left his face, but Valanor said, "No doubt, but it's different for us. A man goes, a half-orc doesn't—he gets signed away like an ox or an ass."

"I don't—"she began again, then hesitated, frowning. "Aye, there was a parchment, now you mention it, something to do with his willingness to go. They pushed it under my nose, I made my X." She shrugged.

As she spoke, Valanor's single black eyebrow edged

upward, then sharply down. "You made your X," he echoed, his hands sliding together to rest upon the deck. "You can't read."

The uneasy feeling returned to her guts, and Joenna waited, watching him, her good hand tucked between her knees.

"They must have seen it, those men who came to your house," he murmured, his eyes searching the distance.

"Seen what? Valanor, I'm not with you."

"Aye, I know." He kept his face turned. "That paper you signed, it wasn't a volunteer roster. Under the law, any orcish child is considered the property of its parent—not unusual, just more formal than for full-blood children. That paper you signed was a transfer of ownership giving your son to the king, relinquishing your rights and responsibilities. Did I say we're treated like oxen or asses? No, if you sold an animal, at least you'd've gotten the money to show for it."

"No," she said, and the sleepers stirred at her tone, so that she lowered her voice again, and pulled herself closer to him. "No, Valanor, I never. I would never—" Biting off the words, she clamped shut her eyes and mouth.

His voice more gentle—if it could ever be called that—Valanor said, "That's why I wondered. You played at being the good mother, you came all this way to avenge him. How could you give him away? It didn't occur to me that you didn't know. Most of our parents, they were happy to see us go. The army was supposed to explain that paper to those who couldn't understand it, but when they came to you," he gulped, and paused, before he continued, "they must have seen you loved him. It must have been a shock, a revelation that any mother could love such a son."

"It weren't his fault, what he was," she murmured, her thoughts turning inward, back to the day they parted, how she stifled her tears until he'd marched away in the company of those soldiers, proud to finally be of service even if it killed him. "It weren't mine, either," she added, "that's why we got on so well, I think."

Resting back upon the slats, Valanor stared at the high clouds. "Aye," he said. "Your story is so strange to me, like one of those tales my mother used to read about impossible beings and unbelievable things."

"It's true," she growled. "Doubt what you will in this world, but never doubt that I loved my son, and I've got the notches to prove it." She gripped the ax at her side, feeling the five new marks she had carved that morning.

"You were right—I don't know how a mother should act—I barely knew mine." He let out a long, low breath, and finally faced her again. "Yes, she was a daRives, a duke's daughter. The king's minister of War was her husband." He became fascinated with wood grain between his feet, tracing it with a curving fingernail. "I heard none of this from them," he murmured. "Got most of it from servants and rumors. She must have been very young, newly married, living at her father's home while her husband dealt with royal business. Her husband came to call on his way back to the border-lands to deal with the orcs. They made love—they must have, or—"he broke off, swallowing, and was silent for a few turns of the tall wagon wheels.

Joenna waited, barely breathing. She kept her jaw clenched, knowing what she was about to hear, already hearing the echoes in her own memory, and her own body, no longer young.

"She read all the time," Valanor said at length. "Her favorite place was the garden, this sort of country part where the formal pathways rambled off and became woodland trails. They placed benches and gazebos around the bends, like a treasure hunt, and she had one gazebo in particular where she brought her stories. It has a peaked roof that's painted inside with legends. Well," he amended, "one legend, my namesake.

"She might have heard them coming, but it was raining that day—"

Raining hard, Joenna thought, down in her little village, but it didn't matter, you still had chores to do, cow to milk, butter to churn over in the community barn. The barn's tin roof sounded like the drums of war, with all that rain, and it flowed down from the eaves so that a girl might long to stay under, rather than go out into the water.

"—orcs can still track in the rain, better sometimes, if the wind is right. They tore up the book and scattered its pages before they—"

They upset the milk jugs she had set down by the open-end of the barn, and they stomped through the mud to get to her. Four of them, but she could hear now the terrible crashing as others broke down doors, and distant screams as they took what they would. When they were through with her, they left her lying in the mud as they drove away the cows.

"—made love because otherwise, she'd have taken something, wouldn't she? But she couldn't be sure the baby wasn't her husband's, so they had to wait. Most of the pregnancy, she lay abed, still recovering from the beating they gave her—"

Joenna wept that night for the beating her parents gave her, somehow convinced she had brought on the attack, or should, at the very least, have saved the milk or the cow, or, failing even that, have come directly home, despite the rain.

"—knew the minute my head came through. The midwife still shudders when she speaks of it. They nursed me with sheep's milk. The gods only know why they bothered—"

Giving birth alone had been the worst of it, Joenna lying in the little shack she had found, screaming aloud from the pain and the loneliness. She knew a few things about birthing from tending the cows, but she didn't expect it to hurt so much. The baby cried, too, and she cradled him close in her arms, and brought him to her breast, and she wasn't alone anymore.

"—grew up in the kitchens, with a few orphans, and a few of the scullery's children. My mother lived for years after that, but she never left her bed again, she never recovered. I used to sneak up the service stairs and sit outside her door to listen to the stories they read to her, and I wished I could be like the heroes, and find a way to make her well. I had done this to her—"

Loref learned fast about the forest plants, and how to use a bow to bring down the creatures he could track better than any. She sold the hides in a nearby village, where nobody knew her, and bought a few sheep, and better shoes for her son's enormous feet.

"—the story of Valanor. I had to get it from the other children, and I tried to find the garden house where it was painted on the ceiling, but it's not there anymore. You can just see the barren patch of ground where something used to be. They let me follow the others to school, if I stayed quiet—"

She'd bought him a new ax—an ax longer and stronger, made for a man--not long before the army came, and took him away.

"—when being quiet didn't help." His sharp nail carved a little hollow into the wood. "The army never came to daRives. My mother's husband brought me away, with a few others rounded up in the neighboring villages. It was the first time I knew there were others." Shaking back his shaggy hair, Valanor regarded her.

"I'm sorry," she told him, her sympathy mingled with a sudden warmth as she thought on her time with her own boy. She wondered how her own story came to be so different from his mother's; how many times in those years had she longed for the comfort of a real home, the security that wealth could buy, and yet she regretted not a moment she had spent with Loref, nor even, now that she looked back on it, did she regret that she had had him. Then she knew why the stories were different, and why she sat in this wagon, clad as a man, going off to do battle with demons. "You couldn't heal her, Valanor—she had to decide to heal herself."

He gave a bitter laugh. "Aye, well, even the Valanor of old could not have done, had he ridden from the Sunset Hills with the golden chalice of Ishdren and the velvet cloak of Athanel, and every other treasure he ever won. My mother had treasures aplenty, and heroes of her own, and they all came to naught."

Aye, Joenna thought, because she knew not what to treasure, but she kept her peace and they rode on, eventually falling asleep to the clump-clump of hoof beats and the creak of the wheels.

CHAPTER

FIVE

Battle's End

FOR THE NEXT BATTLE, JOENNA divided her force into three parts, adding the few local scouts. Now that they knew the scent, they moved with purpose among the enemy, slashing with those enormous swords.

When they heard the horns announcing the army's arrival, Valanor and Joenna drew together, letting the horsemen and archers flow past, cheering. They gave each other a slow glance, taking stock, and finding that neither was wounded, they shared a grin. Then Valanor's gaze fell back to the ax, resting head-down by Joenna's boots. "How many notches?"

Joenna followed his gaze, counting the marks in the bloody handle. She lacked but two. Two more notches made Loref's years, the count she had promised herself, and sworn upon his unknown grave. Twenty-one marks, then she could go home. Her left shoulder ached, and she reached up to support the elbow. The ache pulsed through her body, taking up residence in her hips and knees, not to mention the strong right arm, weary from swinging her ax for hours to cleave the flesh of Demons. Her breasts, too, ached, imprisoned behind the armor plate that guarded her heart, and concealed her secret. Two more notches and she could go home, turning her back on all of this, finding a way to start a new life.

"Well?" he prompted.

Joenna stared at the handle of her ax, then lifted her eyes to the half-orc before her, and the dozen others making their way back to her command. She looked up into Valanor's face. "None."

"What?" His wide mouth twisted with the word. "You killed at least four, by my count, and I got distracted toward the end, so there's got to be more."

Ruffling a hand through her hair, Joenna shrugged. "Naw. None at all, no marks."

"It can't be," he muttered, "I saw them fall, at least four—no, five."

She stood her ground. "Sorry to disappoint you."

With a soft laugh, Valanor leaned on his sword. "No, Joenna, you've not disappointed me—you'll have to try a lot harder for that."

At the roll-call, she found that she had lost four more of her original band, but the remaining troops no longer resented her leadership, or most of them, anyhow, for Koresh always managed to get in his darts. They marched back to the camp, letting the regiment of men mop up the battle, and plunged immediately into the near-by river to wash away the scent of death that clung alongside the gore.

For a moment, Valanor and Joenna stood watching, he checking the bandage on her arm, then he rolled a shrug from one shoulder to the other, and sprinted down to dive in himself. From here, they looked like a school full of boys, let out on a summer morning to splash and play—except when they were done, the river would flow red.

Joenna wiped the gore from her own breastplate, and the sweat from her forehead, then glanced down at her hands and frowned. How long had it been since she'd had a bath? Blue Lady—she must smell like a mizzen pit to the sensitive half-orcs. Crossing to the tent she'd been given, Joenna stripped off her armor. She took some time to bind her breasts before replacing her shirt and marched down to the river.

Her soldiers gathered in the water in little knots of their friends, long arms gesturing as they spoke. "—and then I pulled a dagger," Brion was telling Valanor, reliving the moment, "and shoved it in up to the hilt. By the Gods, it was the biggest demon I ever—"he broke off, jaw working on air, as Joenna approached.

Sweeping them with her gaze, she plopped down on a stone and yanked off her boots. "Sorry, lads, those're too good to soak." With a grin and a nod, she leapt into the pool, and came up snorting and shaking her hair.

To a man, the half-orcs stared, white edges showing around black eyes.

Ducking under and coming up again, Joenna frowned at

them. "Well, y're always washing off the filth—can't imagine I smell much better to you than all of that, eh?"

"Aye," Koresh snarled. "That's because you're not one of us, and no amount of washing will make you so."

"Why, Koresh, you make it sound like I'm missing out."

He leaned down, dwarfing her, his head a dark mass against the brilliant day. "I don't know what you want from this false friendship, sergeant, but you'll not get it from me. You're just another full-blood looking for the chance to bring us down."

Joenna cocked her head as if she were considering it. "D'you think I could?"

"Not bloody likely," Koresh spat into her face.

With a shrug, Joenna tread water for a moment, then turned from him. As she did so, she hooked one foot around his knee and propelled herself away.

He came down with a tremendous splash and came up again with a roar, only to find his fellows laughing. They laughed as Joenna had never heard them before, a cacophony of high hysterics and low grunts of amusement that bordered on pain. Slapping their palms on the water, doubled over, they laughed. Smothering his grin, Valanor waded closer, not quite between them, but near enough to be of use as Koresh balled his fists, emitting a growl.

Rogan caught Koresh's arm. "Sergeant's little, but he's tougher than he looks, eh, Kor?"

"Aye," Koresh muttered. "He'll have to be, or he won't even hear me coming."

"Leave off your threats, Koresh, Joseph's not about to

betray us," Valanor said, "and yes, he's a lot tougher than you know."

"If he thinks it'll get him in with daRives to be your friend than he's stupider than he looks, too."

"Open your eyes, Koresh! He's going to get us out of this war alive, as many of us as he can. If you're wise, you'll stick close and be one of the survivors."

Grabbing Rogan's hand, Koresh wrenched it free and shoved him away, pulling himself up. "If he's so tough, why can't he fight his own battles."

Joenna swam over, her feet barely brushing the bottom in a place where they all stood at ease, and said, "I can, Koresh, and I've got the ax the prove it. But you won't lay a hand on me, not now." She gave Valanor a nudge, feeling his resistance, but urging him out of the way. Reluctantly, he stepped aside, and gave her a clear path to Koresh.

"What makes you think that, little man?"

"Because you'll either win or you'll lose. If you lose, you'll die: that's easy enough for the rest of us. But if you win, the army'll come down on you so hard there won't be enough left of you to scrape into a barrel, and they won't let it go at that, will they? They'll take down Valanor 'cause they think he's watching my back. Then maybe Rogan, 'cause he's trying to watch yours. Maybe they let the rest live, after a few hours on the barrel or a few broken bones, because they still need some scouts." She drew a deep breath, chilled by the truth of her own words. "Then again, maybe not. War's about over now, maybe the last thing the king wants is you lot roaming free again."

Koresh wore a mask of anger, but his eyes turned wary, flicked to Rogan, and the others, and came back to her. Slowly, he slouched back into his habitual posture. Slowly, a grin spread across his face. "Fine," he agreed, "not now. But the daylight won't last forever." He strode away, his wake churning the silt into whirlpools of anger.

That evening, after sharing in the full-blood's celebration, Joenna slumped back to her tent, her belly stuffed with venison, her left arm throbbing with every step. A tall, gangly shadow hulked beside the canvas, stretching itself as she approached, and Joenna sighed as Valanor rose. She tilted her face to look up at him. "What're you doing here?"

"Watching your back."

"Not wise, Val—the army wants you back with your own. You know what they'll do if they catch you."

"They're too drunk to catch their own jokes. It's you who's in danger."

"You really think Koresh is that stupid?"

"He's that angry—he's like the rest of us, sick of the tyranny and busting to do something about it."

Joenna snorted. "You do use those big words of yours, don't you."

"Joenna, he's dangerous. He might hesitate if he smells me hanging around."

"You sound like somebody's father."

"Aye," he said, "and I'm making sure that the orcs don't come calling, right?"

With a broad gesture, Joenna gave in. "Very well, but I'll not have you punished again on my behalf. I'll tell the officers that you're my man at arms. That's a joke they'll appreciate."

His teeth flashed white through the darkness, and Joenna's heart gave an awkward lurch. Somehow, she knew she would sleep well that night.

Three more battles awaited the company; three battles that saw their numbers dropping from eighteen, to fourteen, to eleven, to nine. They trained the other scouts they encountered, sending them off to harry the last of the enemy in this valley or that field. One morning, a single ox-cart waited to carry them, numb and weary, to the king's own camp, and Joenna realized that the fighting was done, at long last, and she had lost count of the notches she no longer carved. The count stood at nineteen, two shy, but she doubted Loref would mind.

All too soon, the cart came to a halt before a council hall where the King had set up his traveling court. At the herald's behest, Joenna clambered down, feeling every one of her forty-four years, plus a few extra. Her left arm hung stiff at her side, fingers brushing over the head of her trusty ax. Valanor jumped down beside her, little the worse for wear, aside from a few cuts and bruises.

The herald drew back. "They can wait in the cart for further orders."

Joenna planted herself at Valanor's side. "This here's my man at arms, and I'll have him with me."

"Your what?" The man's head tipped back as he gawked at the half-orc.

Valanor grinned down at him.

Gulping, the herald danced a few steps away, flashing

a look to the royal guards, their plumes flapping in an afternoon breeze. "At the very least, he'll have to leave his weapons."

"Don't be daft—what's the point of a man at arms without arms, eh?" she barked at the herald.

"Sergeant," Valanor said, ducking his head, "it is the royal court."

Joenna sighed, nodded, and Valanor unbuckled the strap across his chest, giving his sword into the hands of a royal guard, then handed over his dagger in its sheath. He held back a moment, allowing her to precede him up the broad staircase to the borrowed hall. At the door, she hesitated, squinting into the great room, and stepped over the threshold. The guards to either side muttered behind her, and she turned sharply as Valanor came up.

He ducked to fit his lean frame under the arch, and a booted foot stuck out. Joenna had time for a curse as Valanor went down, stumbling over first the foot, then the raised threshold and sprawling hard onto the stone floor.

"Teach the H'or to keep his place," someone remarked, rooting Joenna, her hand on her ax as she decided if she should strike back.

First, there was Valanor to see to. He lay curled on his side, his shoulders shaking, too still for her comfort. She dropped to one knee beside him. "Val! Valanor, are you alright?"

"Don't," he mumbled, "don't—not here, s-sergeant."

Her fingers dug into the iron of the ax, as she forced herself back into her role. "Hey, get up—it weren't so bad a fall, eh?"

Valanor's hand groped over the floor for a moment, and he pushed himself up, his body still leaning, his breathing ragged. "I'm fine, sir, I'll be fine." His voice trembled, but he shot her that black-eyed glare, and Joenna rose.

Drawing the ax in a quick movement, she rounded on the guards who stuck their heads through the door, enjoying their fun. They jerked back again at the sight of her. "So you've had your fun, you bastards. This is the bloody royal court of his Majesty, King Agravaine and it deserves more respect."

A deep chuckle rolled from the dim space behind her. The guards froze, then withdrew, stamping to attention outside the door. Joenna sneered after them, sliding her ax back into its loop.

Turning on her heel, she found herself face to face—well, face to insignia chain—with a tall, silver-haired man, his eyes sparkling. He spread a bejeweled hand toward her. "So, you must be Joseph, the man we've heard so much about."

"Ah—Aye, sir, that I am." She made a brief bow, her left arm cooperating a little.

"Once more you attempt to defend the court. We should not be surprised, should we, after all the reports we've had of you. Come, come, the king himself is eager to meet you."

"Ah," she said again, and some long-silent part of her wondered how she looked, if she'd truly washed off the battle grime at that last swimming hole and if she looked as stupid as she felt, just then. Maybe when she revealed herself, her heroism could--Joenna snapped shut her jaw and cursed herself for a fool: it was no good suddenly feeling womanish when everyone here thought she was a man. Still and all, she'd not seen a face like his in a good long age, and his smile spoke of a lifetime's pleasures.

Something scraped on the floor alongside, and Joenna shook herself. "Aye, sir, thank you. I just need to see to my man."

The handsome face stilled, and Joenna's heart sank. She'd done something wrong already; how like her, to disappoint him when they'd only just met, and he'd heard those good reports about her and all. The bright eyes flicked down, then back up, and her spirits fell yet lower. "Your. . . man. . . has said he is fine. Why not leave him to it?"

Joenna felt her cheeks flare and ducked, rubbing her hand down her face as if merely exhausted. She let her eyes edge back up the stranger's garments, a long robe of deepest blue, such a match for those eyes, and it displayed the chain of his office to excellent advantage. The chain, his office. Joenna blinked and squinted, and her mood changed from fancy to fury.

Knotting her fists, Joenna shoved down the anger: it was as she had said, the king's own court, not the place for confrontations, certainly not for a confrontation that did not even belong to her.

"Just a moment, sir," she said, her voice strong and steady now. "I need to see to my man."

She wrenched her gaze from the Minister of War, and turned to Valanor, who knelt behind the first row of benches, his head still bowed and his right arm pressed against his chest.

"Blue Lady!" In two steps she stood before him, their heads almost level, and touched his shoulder. "Val," she said, "is it broken?"

"Aye," he rasped. "I put out my hand." He gasped a sharp breath. "Stupid."

"We'll get you a surgeon, right now."

"You've been called to court," he mumbled. "Don't keep the king waiting."

Behind her, the Minister cleared his throat, and tapped the toe of a suede slipper.

"That's him, isn't it?"

"Aye."

"Ah, bloody bones and demons," she said, squatting down, and gratified to earn herself a breathy chuckle.

"You just come up with that, Sergeant?" he sighed, finally raising his eyes. They shone with unshed tears, his wide mouth trembling at the corners.

Unscathed, she had thought him, not so long ago, but lines etched his strange, young face and she could see the darkness under the sallow skin. "Great Gods, but it's been a long war."

He mustered a twitch of a smile. "Aye."

"Come on, come up with me—there's room at the front."

Clutching his arm, the hand stuck at an off angle, Valanor shook his head, his eyes flicking again toward the aisle, and the man waiting in it. "I can't."

"You can face a hundred demons before breakfast, Val, you can do this."

"What are you two speaking of so earnestly?" said a languorous voice, and the handsome face appeared near hers as the Minister bent down beside her. "Oh, it is broken? I'm sure there's someone nearby who can wrap it up—there's bound to be a man for the horses at any rate. Would you like me to fetch a page to bring him there?"

"No," Joenna snarled, "I would not."

The tone arrested his expression somewhere between solicitude and disdain, and Joenna had never seen anything so ugly. It shifted quickly to the proper face, and he spoke again. "I dare say you have become. . . close, during these months of fighting, but really, Sergeant, it's time to return to the world of men, and let the rest be what they are, don't you think?"

The fingers of her left hand flexed along the notches of her ax-handle. "Aye," she said at length, "I do. Come on, Val."

"Sergeant, the minister is right, I—"

"Come on, Val—should I make it an order?" She met his worried gaze, and murmured, "You don't have to hide in the kitchen any more."

With a swallow, and faint nod, Valanor braced his left hand on the floor and got his feet under him, rising slowly to his full height, his right hand kept close to his chest. For a moment, he swayed, then steadied. Nodding again, Valanor said, "I've got your back."

CHAPTER

SIX

Royal Progress

THE MINISTER, TOO, ROSE, HIS fine eyes narrowed, raking along Valanor's body like a bear claws a tree, then he smiled again, and turned to lead them on. They marched between the two rows of benches, curious eyes following them the length of the room until they stood before the throne, a portable affair of solid oak. The king himself rose at their approach, and his minister stepped aside with a sweeping gesture and a lift of his eyebrows to usher them into the royal presence.

King Agravaine was of an age with his minister—not much older than Joenna herself, and she recalled when his mother had died, leaving him the throne. Even in her lonely little valley, they'd heard the news. Tall and fair, Agravaine had a mane of golden curls that draped the shoulders of his purple tabard. Underneath, he wore chain mail with the glint of silver that has never known a sword, and a crowned helmet sat beside his feet.

Joenna gave a low bow, and sank to her knees. She heard the stifled cry as Valanor followed suit just to her left and behind. Damn the royal guard, she thought as she faced the king, then she lost the thought as she realized that he was bowing to her. Her!

"Joseph," the king intoned. "My general swears to me that without your charge, the demons would yet be over-running our nation. Your plan was bold and brave, fool-hardy, it might appear to others, to bring ill-trained half-monsters onto the field as a vanguard for an army, and yet, due to your leadership, the plan succeeded. It is rare indeed that any soldier shows such valor, rarer yet that the soldier in question has fought for only a few months, and only under the burden of such grief as the loss of a son. You are a remarkable man, Joseph, and I am honored to have you in my service." Again, he bowed, and a cheer rose up from the rows of people behind her.

"As my first gesture of the gratitude of the crown, and of the people of Corsevale, I would do this." With a gentle curve of his hand, he invited the herald to take over.

The herald, having regained his composure, stepped up, a slender sword lying across his palms. "The sapphire sword of Corsevale, mark of a Knight of the Realm." He lifted it over his head, turning slowly for the admiration of the crowd, then bent on one knee to hold it out to Joenna.

The sword glittered under candle-light, its steel sending

up sparks of flame as the herald shifted. The simple hilt swept into a curving pommel which bore a single large stone, a gleaming lump of blue as deep as the Minister's eyes. That stone, Joenna realized, could have bought the village she grew up in, and its cattle, too. When she got back, maybe that's just what she would do. Grinning madly, she reached for the sword, taking it onto her own palms, her left hand shaky but obedient.

"And this," the herald continued, "to show all who meet you that you are a man of extraordinary worth." He again raised his hands, this time unreeling a length of blue cloth that whispered between his fingers. He held it out for a moment, head bowed to acknowledge Joenna's service, then slipped it around her waist, just under the breastplate, wrapping the ends into a careful knot. "Wear them with pride." Bowing again, he rose and withdrew.

Joenna mumbled, "I will." Her fingers closed around the warm blade and brought it close. She, Joenna, a Knight of the Realm. Wouldn't her parents be. . . stunned. Desperately, she forced her un-manly giggles into a sort of cough instead, then she glanced up. "Thank you, Your Majesty. You truly can't know what this means to me."

The king beamed down at her, his hands spread. "You are a knight of my crown, Joseph, and I am beholden to you for all that you have done—"

"But I did not do it alone," she said, thrusting up her chin.

Silence struck across the room like the moment between thunder and lightning.

"Will you give such honor to my men, your Majesty?"

The king's smile stretched a little thin as his eyes flickered to her left, and the Minister leaned close to his ear to whisper.

Staring up at them, Joenna felt the sword biting into her palms and she loosened her grip, then slid the blade home into a loop beside the ax, both weapons resting awkwardly on the floor.

At last, the two men separated. With a nod, the smile returning, King Agravaine said, "But, Joseph, I have not finished with you yet."

"I need no more honor than this, your Majesty," she said, dredging up the words from somewhere, suspecting a tactic to distract her from her purpose.

"This is not an honor," he said, furrowing his brow, "it is a duty, a great responsibility." He waved his hand at the herald again, and the man brought out a scroll, a creamy parchment wrapped several times around an ornate staff longer than the sword they'd already given her. "As you know, Joseph, many of our citizens fell in this war, both the men who fought it, and the women who bravely defended their homes. Many lords and nobles, too, were slain by demon swords. It leaves the kingdom in a bit of disarray, as it were. So many villages empty, so much farmland untended, but whom to trust with the task of re-building?"

The king smiled more gently. "I am given to understand that your own home—what was its name?"

Kneeling there before him, listening to the pretty speech, Joenna simmered. She cocked her head a little to the left and stared into the king's face. "Lorefsdam."

Valanor smothered a snort of laughter, but the king merely arched an eyebrow. "I regret that I don't recall having visited there."

"It was a very small place, Your Majesty."

"Indeed. So, Joseph of Lorefsdam, where was I? Ah, yes, it was destroyed, was it not? I have estates in need of masters, and worthy warriors such as yourself in need of homes." He reached out to tap the scroll with one finger. "This scroll contains the deed to lands and buildings of Glamshire, at the shores of Lake Muskraven, within the bounds of the Viceroyalty of Goshan, and I should be well-pleased if you consent to be my sheriff there. You may take possession immediately, and I shall include in the grant horses to carry you there. The place is, I tell you candidly, not in good repair, and you have no citizens yet, save those you may recruit."

Lands, village, manor—sheriff? Joenna's mouth felt dry. "I am," she began, "I'm, ah, overwhelmed, your Majesty."

The words won her another miraculous beam, like sunshine let into the hall, and the herald dropped to one knee, offering the scroll. Joenna's hand trembled as she took it. "Thank you, your Majesty," she managed.

"You'll want to study that before you leave, to be sure you understand the meaning, then I will ask for your signature."

The heavy thing filled her hands, and she bowed her head over it. "Do you mind, that is, can I take it outside, where the light's better?"

A ripple of laughter ran the room, with the Minister's marvelous chuckle filling in as well, and the king gave a brief bow of dismissal. "Take your time, Sheriff."

"Yes, thank you." She rose to her feet and turned, walking slowly down the aisle, remembering to bow somewhere near the second row, and then kept walking until she reached the sun.

CHAPTER

SEVEN

New Orders

DUCKING VERY CAREFULLY, HIS TEETH bared, Valanor followed her out into the glare of late afternoon. She glanced sidelong at him. "Read it with me?"

He nodded, motioning toward the far side of the stairs, and they went to sit down, staying quiet for a while before she unrolled the scroll. "Upside down," he said, and she turned it over, holding it out before him as Valanor read.

"Unto all by whom these presents come, does his glorious and wrathful Majesty, King Agravaine of Corsevale, send his most regal greetings," Valanor began, then hesitated, catching his breath, and Joenna frowned.

He sat very still, his left hand trembling slightly in his lap. As if he felt her eyes upon it, Valanor curled it into a fist, stilling even that movement. "Sorry," he mumbled, drawing his attention back to the document, but Joenna let it go, the parchment re-curling of its own accord, and slapped it down on the step.

"Great Gods, Val, you must think me an ass! There I sit, all a-tremble like a little girl, and you've got a broken wrist to worry you, and now I'm making you forge through this ridiculous thing—"she broke off with a sigh and stuck out her hands. "Give it over."

Darting her a glance, Valanor complied, lowering his right arm, the swelling wrist resting lightly on her palm, and he winced at even that contact.

Joenna bent her head over the task, running her fingers gently over the break. It was a simple one, praise the Lady. "Ought to get this popped back in place, before it can heal right." If it ever will, she thought. "I'll go for that doctor."

"Can you do it?"

"I've only ever done cows and sheep," she said, "and if it went wrong, we had mutton."

Offering a wan smile, he pointed out, "You think a horse doctor can do it better?"

"Must be a real one around someplace, town this size." She squinted out over the streets, but he gave a little laugh, and she squinted at him instead.

"Real doctor won't see me. Did you see the army surgeons come for us, all those months?"

"Damn," she said again, with feeling. "It'll hurt bad, I warn you, but it might feel some better when it's done."

"Aye, well, I'll have to hope so."

Nodding once, she adjusted her hold, taking his hand

firmly in her own, arranging herself with her back to him, her arm laid alongside his, ready. "I'll take it quick," she said, "and you promise not to fall off the steps, or knock my head off, right?"

"Right—holy fathers!" for she had applied herself with that combination of twist and massage, and only hoped she'd done it well enough. She felt the tension that shot through his powerful arm, but she, too, had grown strong in her time of hewing demons, and she held him, his hand rough and enormous in her grasp. Warm and damp with sweat, it felt like any other hand as she studied the clawed fingers that clenched against hers, recalling how one of those talons had scraped her very solid breastplate. Dark curly hair trailed from his sleeve cuff all the way down to his knuckles, thinning out some around the joints. The joints of her own fingers knobbed out against the work-tanned flesh, the skin chapped and cracked, showing more pale toward the palm. Her thumb, calloused from gripping the handle of her ax, rubbed gently against his skin, and his cursing slowly evaporated, along with some of the tension. Bruising darkened the wrist, and it thickened with swelling, but she thought it would be alright.

Releasing him, lowering his hand to rest along her leg, Joenna unwound the sash from her waist, yanking apart the elaborate knot. She wrapped the middle of it loosely over his arm and finally turned back to him, her face at the level of his chest. Looping the ends about his neck, she made a simple knot of her own and scooted back along the stone to look up at him.

Valanor stroked long fingers down the brilliant blue of the cloth, resting them for a moment on his swaddled wrist. "King's not going to like that," he murmured.

"Not my concern, is it—he's already given his grant, eh?" She grinned and waggled the scroll.

"Don't trust nobles," said Valanor against his chest.

Down in the street, something crashed, and voices shouted.

The oxcart which had brought them lay on its side, the oxen lowing their confusion as the eight remaining half-orcs clustered near, back to back, their swords drawn. Archers surrounded them, and swordsmen in the tunics of the king's army. "Bloody Blue Lady!" Joenna launched herself down the stairs two at a time, the scroll raised up to her shoulder like a brickbat. "What's going on? What're you about with my men?"

"Stand down, Sergeant," said one of the soldiers. "We've got orders."

"What kind, from whom? The war's over, isn't it?"

"Aye, well, they've recalled all this lot for some new training. As you can see, they're resisting."

She could see, too, the chains and manacles dangling from the soldiers' belts. "There's no re-training," she said, more slowly as she tried to figure it out, "it's time to go home."

"Most of them aren't wanted back, are they? They're in the army, now, there's other work for them to do."

"In chains?"

At that, the man stiffened, and lost his air of camaraderie. "If they resist turning over their weapons, aye, they go in chains. And we've got a stinkpot on the way, for a little extra encouragement."

"Whyn't we hear of this earlier? Why now, and here?" But she knew as Valanor's shadow fell alongside hers. Joenna swept her eyes over the half-orc huddle, their bruised and weary faces framing eyes that flashed with dread. Thrusting her scroll in the soldier's face she said, "Don't kill anybody." Then she shouted at Koresh, "And that goes for you, too!"

She turned back and flung herself up the stairs. Leaping the threshold, she charged up the aisle, and the new supplicant, a soldier like herself, threw himself to one side to avoid being run down. "What's going on? Your Majesty, they're trying to clap my men in chains!"

King Agravaine arched an eyebrow. "Your men?"

The Minister of War leaned over and whispered, and the king nodded. "You are referring to the half-orcs assigned to you. Yes, well, they are to be re-assigned. The war may be done, but there is still the cleaning up, and sniffing out the last of the demons, not to mention whatever other magical traps and creatures may be lurking. We have need of creatures of our own."

"They've been in active combat for months—over a year, some of them! They need rest, and medical aid."

"Some of them need a bath," the Minister remarked, drawing laughter from the room.

"They're a lot cleaner than some," Joenna muttered.

With his glowing smile, the Minister said, "I don't believe you understand their situation, Joseph—or shall I call you sheriff?—in any event, they are here because nobody wanted them back home, you see? They don't choose to go here or there like real men, they belong to the king and there are papers to that effect, duly signed and witnessed by the people who donated them."

The words struck at her like darts, finding the sore wound of her grief and jabbing in. "You can't just drag them off," she insisted.

Still smiling, the Minister stepped down from the dais he shared with the king and paced over to face her directly. He lay a hand upon her shoulder. "I may not look it, Joseph, but I have known combat, as you have. I know that there are. . . relationships, forged upon a battlefield which would never be, under ordinary circumstances—knights with footmen, nobles with spear-carriers. I understand all of that, but it's done now, the war is over, and it's time for each to return to his place, and fulfill the roles given to him. In your case, due to your extraordinary bravery, you have earned a new place." The smile widened, and he squeezed her shoulder to show his encouragement.

"And so have they," she said. "It was not done alone."

"The trouble is," he said, his hand becoming heavy, "that you keep talking as if they were men, like you and me, and they are not."

Nor am I, she wanted to snarl, but she felt the slightest touch on her elbow, and found Valanor, face averted, kneeling beside her. He gave a slight shake of the head, and she gritted her teeth, then shouted, "That's where you're wrong, Sir— Valanor's a better man than I am, on any field!"

The Minister flinched, his eyelids fluttering down, and

his hand fell away from her. "Ah, Joseph," he murmured, his voice thick with emotion. "You don't know how you have wounded me." He swallowed, his throat working for a moment, then he leaned near her—the way that he spoke to the king himself—and whispered, "My own dear wife was taken by the brutes when they raided. She was barely seventeen, so lovely—when her face wasn't hidden behind a book." A tiny chuckle slipped from his lips, but they trembled as he spoke. "If I had been there, Joseph—Gods, I'd have ripped their heads off before they laid a hand upon her. It killed her, what they did to her. To say that any spawn of such a rape is even barely human is to defame the women they tortured, Joseph." He pressed his fist to his lips, his deep eyes unfocused.

As he spoke, Joenna found herself back upon that day, the rain slamming against the roof as the hideous creature grunted over her, its breath slapping her face with every movement, and tears coursing down her cheeks. She lay there unable to scream for the huge hand that stopped her mouth, the hairs on the back of it tickling her into madness even as she swore she must be dying. When she looked on Valanor, she saw someone like her own son—the beloved product of that awful afternoon—but the Minister saw the very physical embodiment of the monsters who mauled and murdered his wife, equally beloved.

"I'm sorry," she whispered. "I never saw it that way."

"Yes," he answered. "I don't often. . . that is, most don't know this." His fine features bent as he tried to ask it, but Joenna knew what he wanted, and she nodded.

"No, sir, of course. They'll not learn it from me."

"Thanks." The Minister straightened, wiping a hand over his face to erase the marks of his own grief—it almost succeeded. "You are a good man, as we've heard." He glanced to the side, and sighed. "Let me see what I can do."

Lifting the edge of his robes, he returned to the dais. "Your Majesty does, of course, need to maintain the assets of the nation." With a backwards gesture, the Minister said, "This half-orc is Joseph's especial companion. Perhaps you might see your way clear to signing it over to Joseph, for whatever purposes he requires assistance in the new Shire. Besides--"the hand rose into a shrug—"it won't be much use to us with that broken arm."

"Mmm," the king nodded. "Good point. Scribe, write up a transfer deed to Joseph for one half-orc. Put some description." He waved his hand to fill in the details, and the scribe scratched his pen over a small square of parchment, then offered it to the king, who made a few flourishes of his own. A stick of sealing wax dripped on the bottom and the king stamped his seal into it, then the scribe handed it over.

Side by side on the dais, the king and his Minister stood, both smiling, the one with relief, the other with that twinge of memory, his blue eyes still distant.

Joenna took the thing in two fingers, barely feeling the parchment as her stomach sank. She felt sick and hollow at the same time as she stared at the deed between her fingers. Her dry throat refused to work, but she choked out, "Thank you, Your Majesty."

Stiffly, she bent at the waist, then raised her eyes again

to the pair as the king resumed his throne and the Minister turned away, his hand to his face. "Come on," she whispered, and heard the creak of leather as Valanor rose to follow.

When they reached the steps, the setting sun blazed from behind them, lighting their way with red, except for the two jagged shapes of their shadows, both enormous as they stained all the way to the street. The cart and oxen were gone, and her men along with them as she had known they must be. A few spatters of blood marked the place where they had been—not enough that anyone had died there—thank the Lady!

She stared down at the scuffed street, the hoof-prints of the startled oxen, the streaks of blood, a broken arrow, a long drag line through the dirt that made her think of Koresh, refusing the aid of even his own feet. The bile burned her throat and she smashed her scroll against her thigh, the deed clenched in her fist. "The bastards. I'll kill them all! I swear I'll shove this scroll down their throats and hack their heads off with my bloody ax! May the gods rip them to shreds and feed them to worms."

Spinning on her heels, Joenna mounted the steps a third time, her tired knees creaking. "I'm going back in there and make them see!"

An enormous, hairy hand caught her arm. "No."

The memory swept over Joenna and she shouted, slamming the arm with the only weapon she had. Immediately, the remorse followed and she turned, almost the same height as he on the narrow step. "Gods, I am sorry, but I'll make them accept you if I have to—"

"Don't you dare!" he roared. "Don't you dare."

Joenna froze, agape. Valanor stood below her, both hands now held to his chest, the left one forming a fist that could knock her senseless. The crimson glow of sunset lighted his cauldron eyes with fire and glinted red upon his teeth.

"You will not do a thing," he said, his voice now rolling in a wave against her. "You will shut your mouth and walk away, and take yourself to the shire the king himself has given you. Do you hear me?"

"But," she began, and words failed her, so she shook her head. "But why, Val? Gods, all I want is to help you, all of you."

His shoulders drooped, and he let out a long breath of his anger. "You will, Jo, I know that. Right now, you're the only voice we have—the only person who ever dared to think of us as men. The king is building you a bridge. The godsdamned Minister of War told you his side—don't burn those things today, please, Jo. You are all that we have."

His words sank into her skin, tingling against her fury, and she let it dissolve beneath them, her eyes searching his face. He no longer looked frightening, the voice of an angry people, but smaller, more exhausted, younger, too.

Joenna stood there, eye to eye with him for the first time. After a moment, she stuck the deed for her shire through her belt, and slowly looked down at the other fist. "They gave you to me," she whispered.

"Aye," he said, his voice barely audible. "Like an ox or an ass."

"The man who should have been your father," she sighed,

shaking her head. "He must know who you are."

His voice cracked then. "Aye." His chin falling to thump his chest, he broke into sobs, as if his heart were broken, and Joenna realized that it probably was.

The weight of the day and the moment seemed to bear him down. Valanor crumpled to his knees, his forehead pillowed on a marble step, shoulders shaking.

Blinking fiercely, Joenna sank down beside him. "You'll be alright," she whispered. Silently, she prayed to the Lady to make it so.

CHAPTER

EIGHT

Words and Deeds

AFTER A WHILE, AFTER SHADOWS had been consumed by growing dusk, Valanor steadied himself and sat up, glancing at Joenna from under his heavy brow. "I'm sorry," he sighed. "All of this just. . . " he trailed off, ruffling a hand through his hair.

"I know." She leaned back, stretching her spine and massaging her aching shoulder, and thought of the long flight of stairs behind her. "Val," she said.

"Yes?"

"I need to go back in there."

Ferociously, he shook his head. "No, haven't you been listening?"

She held up both hands. "Aye, hush. I won't upset them, I swear by Loref's grave." Wherever that was.

The oath stilled his protest. "What're you up to, Sargeant?"

"I've been thinking." Staring at the splatters of blood, wondering how to help him, and his kin. "And I've got a plan I think'll do it, but it will take time, and another of these pieces of paper they keep handing out." She held up the square that deeded Valanor to herself. "I hate to ask it," she said, taking a deep breath. "But would you read this? All I need to be sure of is, are there any specifics?"

His eyes fell to the parchment, and he read it over, then gave a little snort which might have been laughter. "Yes, they've said that I'm tall, ugly, and have dark hair."

"That's you, that is." Joenna grinned. "I'll be right back, and there won't be any breaking skulls, I promise." She heaved herself up, listening to the protests of aging joints, then slid free her ax and placed it on the step before him. "Still and all, I think you should keep watch on that."

Climbing up the stairs required a special force of will not just for the physical effort, but for going back into that room, facing those men: the king in his pleasant ignorance, the minister in his heart-sick hatred.

The door guard stopped her with a hand. "What happened down there? Seems like your, ah, man at arms, had some trouble, eh?"

"Some," she agreed, "but none of his own making. Speaking of which, I'll be needing back his weapons. The king's signed him over to me."

The guard smirked under his mustache. "I guess a man at arms's no good without arms, eh?" He emphasized the word, and Joenna bristled, reaching for the ax, and finding the king's sword instead.

Slashing it free, she forced the guard to stumble back, thumping against the wall as his companions readied their own arms. "Now don't rush anything," she told them. "I just thought I'd show the man here my new toy." Joenna flipped it up so that the sapphire glittered. "I may not look it, lads, but I'm a Knight of the Realm, and that means I out-rank you lot by a few long steps." She grinned and nodded, acknowledging her own small stature.

With a flourish, she thrust it home again, and raised her empty hands. "So, if you don't want another scene, and I can make'em, then I suggest one of you trot back to the Minister and tell him I need a word."

Joenna stepped inside and leaned against the wall while a muttering guard passed her by and hurried up the aisle. Up front, the herald droned on about something, and a few boys with long sticks tipped by fire prodded the candelabras to life. The guard got the Minister's ear and they came back, still moving fast, hoping to avert the threatened scene.

Joenna allowed herself a smile. Her play-acting got better every day, it seemed. Then the smile wavered as she realized that she'd have to live out the rest of her days as Sheriff Joseph of Glamshire, a stranger in more ways than one.

"What do you want?" The Minister crossed his arms sharply, his brows pinched together over his nose.

Bowing low, Joenna said, "I'm sorry, Gods, but I am sorry to keep bothering you like this, and after all your own troubles you surely don't need more on my account, Sir."

One eyebrow edged upward. "No," he said at length,

"that's true. But you are the king's sheriff now, so. . . what do you want?"

"Well, it's this gift." She waved the square of parchment. "It's real generous and all, and I'm honored, but It's got me a bit worried now, as I think on it. See, folks might not know how to take it, seeing as how the rest of the H'or are being rounded up from re-training, eh? Make it hard for my man to do my errands, see, without people getting up-tight."

The Minister nodded his understanding.

"Then, too, there's accountability, isn't there, Sir? I mean, I'm responsible, and folks ought to know that, in case something happens."

"Which it is bound to, given the nature of the beast, as it were."

She lost sight of his grief for a moment, and nearly snapped, but she gripped that parchment and remembered what was at stake. "Right, see? So I thought you, Sir, might get a scribe to draw up something for him to carry on him, to show people who he is and where he belongs, with a royal seal, you know?"

The Minister bowed his head, his shoulders rising and falling in a gentle rhythm.

Staring up at him, wondering what expressions crossed that handsome, hidden face, Joenna played her fingers over the sapphire sword. It had to work, it simply had to, or she'd have to break her promise to Valanor and break some skulls in any case. This man could make it easy, though he knew it not, but he had little reason to help her, nor to do anything for the half-orc who might have been his son. Joenna's bones felt heavy, her knees longing to give out and let her sleep. They would soon enough, in a bed she hoped, but she had to know that she was doing something, moving in the right direction. Gods, but he thought a long time.

Finally, the silvered head rose and his eyes met hers, nearly as weary as her own, they must be. "Fine. I'll have it done."

Joenna drooped into her exhaustion. "Thank you, Sir. I appreciate all this, truly, I do."

He lifted one hand and twiddled the fingers.

In a moment, a woman with the baldric of a scribe appeared at his elbow, quill and tablet in hand, and he told her what he required. Sitting cross-legged on the floor, she wrote it out, and pressed it with the king's seal. "Anything more, Sir?"

"No, thank you." He graced her with his smile, and she curtseyed as she left. The Minister studied the document a moment, and handed it over. "This should suffice. The horses will be ready for you in the morning, at the Butterpot Inn, if that suits your needs. Tell them who you are, and they'll provide a room for you."

"Again, thank you, Sir. I'm in your debt. Say, daRives isn't far from Glamshire, you come by when we're up and going, and I'll show you some hospitality, eh?" She grinned like a fool, and his eyes widened.

Giving a tight smile, the Minister said, "Yes, well, I'll surely keep you in mind." He made a little bend at the waist, and offered her the door.

Gladly, she took it.

Outside, a guard thrust Valanor's enormous sword into her hands and dropped the dagger on top. "There you are. Anything else we can do for you, Sir?"

"Aye," she said, to his evident irritation. "If I get sick of this H'or, where do I send him for that re-training?"

"Now you're getting smart," he replied, less surly in an instant. "Sycosh Valley's where they've set up camp, I hear. Wish they'd've taken 'em further myself." He waved his hand vaguely north.

"Eh, they have their uses—better than dogs for hunting, aren't they?"

Glancing down the steps to the waiting hulk of Valanor, the guard shrugged. "Never thought of it—more trouble, though."

"Naw," said Joenna, turning away. "People object when you beat a dog."

At that, the guard let out a hoot of laughter. "Aye, well. I guess you're not so bad, then."

As she walked, she gripped her new sword and muttered, "That's 'cause you don't know me well enough." She had half a mind to take up her ax and prove the point, and thanked the Blue Lady she'd had enough wit to leave it behind.

"Are you good to walk?" Joenna asked. "We've got an inn."

"They won't take me," Valanor pointed out, unfolding himself to tower over her in the growing dark. And he was right—they wouldn't, until Joenna threatened to sleep in the barn and tell the king about it in the morning. The room came with several straw pallets, enough for a family, or one half-orc and his new keeper. Joenna gratefully unlaced her breastplate and gave a sigh of relief as she set it aside, then she told Valanor the plan and slowly, patiently defused his objections. She lay down on the rough mattress and listened to the half-orc's vast, low snore. When she shut her eyes, she imagined they were home, in the little shack she had fixed up right, Joenna and her son and his sonorous snoring.

After satisfying herself that Valanor could handle a horse one-handed—to be true, the beast was more like a pony to him—Joenna sent him off down the western road, toward their new home, and turned her mount to the north. On the road, she kicked it into a canter, and soon left the town behind, making a mental note of a side-road that aimed roughly west. Good, excellent.

Her way climbed steadily, then leveled into a plain which afforded good views of the mountains and the way ahead. Not far off, a cloud of dust rose, marking the progress of a company of men. Joenna drew nearer, taking in the remnants of gray tunics that covered their bent backs. They would have dwarfed their wardens, if the full-bloods had not been mounted. For good measure, a pack of huge mastiffs paced alongside, exchanging growls with the prisoners, for prisoners they were, their large hands chained at their throats, with lines strung between to keep the group together. A dozen half-orcs, some limping, some leaving trails of blood from untended wounds.

Joenna clenched her reins so hard the horse snorted and tossed its head, and she forced herself to relax as she came up beside one of the riders. "Hallo, what's all this?"

"Conscripts, for re-training." He cracked a smile. "That's what the general calls it. Far's I know, they're being sent down a mine-shaft—they can see in the dark with those big eyes."

"Aren't they a bit tall for that?"

Shrugging, the soldier replied, "I guess—not really our concern, is it?" With a conspiratorial glance, he leaned to the side, beckoning her to do likewise. "A few've gone crazy in the army, killing their officers, that sort of thing. They're not right in the head, and it's got the king worried. He'll get 'em in the ground one way and another, eh?"

Joenna was saved from answering as one of the half-orcs cried out. He stumbled and fell in his chains, jerking on the others nearby. "Bloody idiots," the soldier snapped, reining in his mount to sort it out. "Get up, you, and I don't want to hear any more of your whimpering!"

Gritting her teeth, Joenna jabbed her heels into the horse's sides and left the company behind.

By the time the sun began to sink, she'd come in sight of the palisade that cut off the mouth of the valley. Turning aside, Joenna hunted around for a good hide-out. She found what she wanted in a narrow defile screened by brush, far enough from the gate and road that the trees would proved cover. That done, she collected her horse and used a rock to re-mount, trotting up to the gate.

"Halt, and state your business," the single guard called out. Joenna smiled to herself—she had come just at mealtime, when the roster was cut and this man would be impatient to get off for his own meal.

"I'm on the king's business. He's given me one of your

workers for hunting out demons 'round my new lands. There was a few scouts from my company I've broken in, as it were, and I figured I take one of those."

"Dismount, and come on over." The soldier waved her through the smaller gate and looked over the paper with a blank expression.

While he perused the document, doing his impression of a literate man, Joenna thought, she got an eyeful of the camp. They had laid out barracks to one side for training during the war, and a broad expanse of open space lay between her and the buildings. Off to one side, smoke rose from cook fires where the full-bloods waited for their meal. Damn, but the place was open. She prayed the plan would work, and counted on the fact that nobody assumed she actually wanted the damned H'or in the first place.

He looked up and handed it back. "Do you know the one you want?"

But Joenna's eye had fallen to the ranks of the half-orcs, among the trees, crouching or lying down, no longer chained, but with the thick bands of metal at their necks and wrists. Her stomach clenched. "How many are there?"

"Right now? Maybe three dozen. We're expecting about that many more—we've got two hundred soldiers just to look after them. Some of us wonder if it's worth the trouble. Just bring the archers down and have done, and the rest of us can go home."

"Aye," she murmured vaguely, for the wind shifted, bringing her an awful stench. She spotted the source immediately—a long pit dug some way down the fence. A lone figure hunched over it, his arms bound up to a frame, tipping him forward over the stink. Even at such a distance, she noticed the sheen of his hair more brown than black, and knew. "Unfortunately, soldier, I think it's that one." She pointed to where Koresh suffered the local version of the stink-barrel.

"That one? He's a real brute—fought us all the way in, and only went limp when we laid into him. You don't want that one."

Joenna started walking that way. "Aye, that's the one. He's the best tracker we had, and good at taking the monsters down. Don't worry," she tossed over her shoulder. "He'll remember me." As they drew near, she could hear Valanor's voice in the back of her head, warning her off, but she couldn't do it. Even Koresh deserved better than this, and she had to start somewhere.

When they drew near, the prisoner flinched, his head lifting slowly at the soldier's shout. He stared at Joenna, his eyes creeping open wider. "Sergeant," he rasped.

"Aye." She stared back, willing him not to ruin everything. "I'm here to take you demon-hunting."

His body shook with silent laughter that broke off in a grunt of pain, letting his head fall back, his hair nearly brushing the surface of the vile sludge. "You've come to take me down again, or see me broken."

Tilting her head, Joenna invited the soldier to acknowledge what he'd heard. "See? No trouble here, not for me. Got the key? I'll let him down."

He pulled one from his belt and handed it over, then

retreated a few steps, covering his nose.

Joenna rounded the pit to the opposite shore and fitted the key to the lock at the half-orc's wrists. With a click and groan, it popped open, and she dropped her arm about his chest before he plunged face-first into the muck. Pushing him back and holding him steady with an appearance of exasperation, Joenna glared down at him. "You up to travel? We've got work to do."

Gasping at the air, Koresh raised sparking eyes to her face and straightened his back until they were almost face to face. "What's this about?" he murmured, his breath reeking of vomit.

"I'll tell you when we're out—meantime, act obedient for the first time in your accursed life."

Again, he flinched, and his eyes shut, two bruises against the gray skin of his face. "Aye, Sergeant. I can walk."

"On your feet then, there's a long way to go before I sleep." She turned away, not bothering to see if he followed, and nodded to the soldier. "So, I'm off. Thanks for your help." She caught her breath as she heard a groan from behind her, then a few careful steps, and a long shadow fell beside hers, slanting toward the gate and freedom.

"Best of luck, Sir," the soldier told her as they left.

"Help me up to the horse," she muttered from the side of her mouth. "Don't worry, I'll give myself a jump."

"Don't worry yourself, full-blood, I'm strong enough yet." He bent down and put his hands together, and she jumped herself up, hearing the sharp hiss of his breath as her weight transferred to the horse.

She turned her mount and headed back to the hidden valley she had found, slithering down again with no help, her back aching. "Damn, this'll be tougher than I thought," she grumbled.

Koresh shuffled through the opening into the ravine, trying to lift his head, the strain in his shoulders still too evident. Stripes of blood marked his bare back and bruises colored his sides.

"Sit down, rest," she told him, bringing out a canteen of water drawn at the last stream.

Turning on her with a snarl, he snatched it from her hands and swayed, his knees buckling. Snarling to herself, she caught his arms and guided him down. "Don't be an idiot, Koresh, I'm trying to help."

"Oh, aye?" he said, after a swallow of water. "Then where's Valanor? What've you done with him?"

"I've sent him home."

"He has no home! Nor have any of us."

"Ye Gods, Koresh, if you'll shut up and stay with me, you will have!" She felt gratified by his compliance, even if he only stopped shouting to drink long and deep. Dropping onto a log, Joenna sighed, "You weren't my first choice, either, but I couldn't leave you where you were, could I?"

"You could," he said around the mouth of the canteen.

"Oh, aye? You could take it all day, all night, too, eh? What a pile of shit, Koresh—I don't know who you think you're fooling."

He glared at her, even as she struck off his chains, as if at any moment she might strike off his hands instead. She pulled herself back up again and collected the horse. "Forget it. I'm going to keep a look out for the change of guards—stay or go, just don't foul it up for the rest of them."

"You planning to smuggle everyone out like that, every man in the camp?"

Her hands gathered the reins, but her heart fell. "You know I can't. The most I can hope for is to get the rest of our company. We'll have to find a way to free the others."

It took three days, waiting for a new man at the gate, taking advantage of meal-times, downpours, the arrival of the new batches, each little group looking more miserable than the last. She found each of her men, giving hope to the ones left behind, stretching her mind for a reason to spring Brion from the infirmary where he languished with infection. Her men—even Koresh—stayed in the ravine, hunting rabbits and tending to each other's wounds. Each time she won, Joenna felt more sick at those she had to leave, all of those strangers who wore her son's face.

At last, she could sit still on her log, looking from one to the next. Young Brion lay huddled against Rogan's side—Rogan, once again the doctor. Dale and Callifrax, the two who could read, admired the document that had freed them. Koresh, still suspicious, watched her in return, waiting for the trap to close. Lassiter, Joram, Shane—the most recent arrival still chugging down more than his share of water, and Dale rising to refill the canteen without being asked.

"What's next, Sergeant? You've got the plan, eh?" Joram asked, with an easy smile.

"We form two lines, you march, I ride, we tell everyone

we meet that we're hunting demons by the lake—we pray to the Blue Lady we don't meet anyone who was at that court where I got my papers. Dunno. I guess that covers it."

Joram tossed his head. "Naw. Missed one thing, at least."

She frowned. "What's that, then?"

"We give thanks to you for saving our lives. Whatever happens next, we owe you for this." He held up his hands, the chain struck off with a stone. "I'm your man, Sergeant, and where you lead, I follow."

"Aye," said Dale.

"And me," echoed more voices, while Koresh merely stared until he was the only one who had not spoken, and everyone else was staring at him.

"I still think you're up to something," he rumbled. "But I'm with you—for now."

Someone laughed, and Lassiter kicked him, and they broke out into the chaos of freedom, splashing water over each others' heads and tossing accusations of faithlessness one way and another. Joenna's grin felt fixed and fragile, and she shoved the heels of her hands against her eyes to keep from crying.

CHAPTER
NINE

Homecoming

THE MARCH TO GLAMSHIRE WOULD have taken about four days, but Brion's fever grew steadily worse, and they stopped as often as they found a stream to bathe him in. After they had passed by the town where the king still held his court— taking the side-road Joenna had spotted—she dismounted, and they strapped Brion on the horse, walking it slow. In support of this action, Joenna muttered loudly whenever they passed another party, especially soldiers, about how she was to round up this lot and drag them all the way to the lake, only the damned lieutenant hadn't mentioned that one of them was sick, and here she was, a bloody sergeant. . . the rant earned her commiseration from most, along with the occasional implication that she was fool to haul a half-dead orc, and wasn't she better off to finish the job. Leaving the company outside a bustling market town, Joenna took the sapphire from her sword hilt—with the help of Joram, who had grown up with metal smiths—and sold it off as a find from her demon-hunting days. They bought a pair of oxen, young, but sturdy, and cart to carry Brion and a few odd tools, plus new daggers for the men. Koresh met Joenna's gaze as he accepted his, and gave a short nod. Still, she knew he was watching, and only hoped the damned thing wouldn't wind up in her own back.

At last, six days after they left the camp, they came up over a rise and passed the tall stone wall that marked the eastern edge of Glamshire. Joenna let the others start down as she gazed at her new home. Her grant spread from here west to the river that marked the boundary of Corsevale, and south to the vast lake. To the north, it climbed rapidly to mountains. In the valley before her, the meadows showed streaks of black and torn ground where there had been fighting, but tufts of grass grew among them, and a few bright daisies glowed beneath the sun. A cluster of rooftops, few still intact, stood not far from where the lake and river met. At the base of the hill, chestnut trees obscured the road, and only the top of a square stone tower showed the manor, at the edge of an open space, but smoke curled up from an unseen chimney, and a knot that had lodged between Joenna's shoulders finally loosened.

Pumping her fist in the air, she whooped for joy, arresting the half-orcs' progress. A few turned back, and their broad faces broke into grins. Callifrax even let out a ululating cry that echoed from the mountains to the lakeside, and they laughed.

"We're home," she whispered to the sky and flowers. There had been moments she thought they'd never make it. Praise the Blue Lady, the defender of the weak, for they had done it.

Joenna trotted down and caught up with her company, leading them on her re-gained horse, a pretty gray mare who would be useful in her own right.

Ancient chestnut limbs obscured the sun for a time, and they emerged again in that clearing, a patch of grassland before the manor. Or what was left of it. The stone tower, remnant of an earlier age, stood at the juncture of two wooden wings perhaps two rooms long, with lofts overhead. One of these looked in good repair, featuring a stone end-wall with a huge chimney and it was from this that the smoke issued. The wing opposite however, stood broken in the middle, its roof yawning to the sky while the walls beneath crumpled into rubble, leaving the end leaning slightly forward, as if gaping at what had happened. Scorch marks traced the damage and darkened one wall as if from a directed blast of fire. Dragon damage.

Joenna slid down from her tall horse, landing with a bump and a curse, to Koresh's amusement.

The door to the intact side stood off its ruined hinges, leaning against the wall, and Valanor appeared in the opening, his right arm bound up in a sling. A toothy grin spread across his face and he bounded down from the stoop to meet them.

"You did it! Joseph, you did it!" As she was about to say

something self-deprecating, joking it off for the benefit of her role, he scooped her up in his single arm and swung her a circle, laughing like a lunatic.

"Put me down, you!" she snapped, trying to sound gruff.

Darting a glance over her head, he smothered his laughter and did as she demanded, stepping back to bend in a more formal greeting. "Sorry."

"Aye, well, ye should be." She clapped a hand to her swinging ax and the sword, now absent its stone.

Valanor bounced among his companions, clasping hands with most, giving Dale a brief embrace, then bending over the oxcart where Rogan checked their still, quiet patient. "What does he need, what can we do?"

"Water," Rogan said. "Soup, maybe, and a few herbs I know of. Let's get him inside—where can we take him?"

"Here, this way." They carried Brion inside, each ducking under the lintel, and Joenna eyed it as she followed. Something would have to be done about that.

As they settled Brion on a pile of straw at a distance from the fire, Shane started to tell the story of their escape, adding his own flair for Valanor's benefit. Listening with half an ear, Valanor directed the unloading of their supplies—flour, sugar, a few spices, a crate full of chickens, some kitchen pots, a delicate case of ink bottles with a packet of quills and a heap of parchment.

Leaving him to it, Joenna strolled around the single large hall that comprised this wing. A narrow staircase at the tower end led up to a sleeping loft above, she gathered, while a door pierced that wall to give access to the tower itself. Along the opposite wall stood a dozen or so pieces of furniture, mostly benches and a few tables, but also two bedsteads with rope lattice to support mattresses. Heaped against the knee-high hearth were all the other bits of civilization Valanor had gleaned from the buildings: a few pots and jugs, some still sealed; boxes and crates of various sizes, most broken; an assortment of children's playthings that made Joenna wonder about the citizens of Glamshire. This close to the border, they must have been attacked early on, maybe even in the first wave of the demon assault. Many would have died that day, and the remaining few fled, taking the things they valued most, leaving this pile behind. What would they think of her plans, she wondered, they who had been invaded by monsters once already?

Turning her back to the piles and the fire, Joenna found Valanor gazing at her from across the room. He directed a few of the others to go for water, and came to squat down before her. "Welcome home, Joseph."

"Aye," she said. "And you. Cor, but it's a pretty spot, eh? Did you ever see the like?"

His smile faded. "I'd like it better were it a little further from daRives."

"Naught to do about that but to keep out of their way, I guess."

"Will do."

"You've been alright?"

"Alright," he agreed, with a half-shrug. "It's not easy, but I've toured the place, rounded up what seemed useful, that sort of thing. Read over the charter."

"And?"

"The usual, I suppose—tithes to the king and the temple, provision of soldiers in time of war, king's protection for yourself and your land. There's some special provisions because we're on the border, like to maintain a border watch that reports to the king. But, likewise, it gives you more freedom of citizenship: you can grant conditional citizenship to anyone you deem worthy. If it stands for a year with no contest, they become citizens."

"A year? Hmm. Can I declare you all citizens?"

"You can try." He cocked his head toward a table by the fire, set up with jugs of water and benches—all a little short for her company, of course, but a good height for her, if he sat on the floor. The royal charter lay on the table, held open by a few lumps of carved stone. "When they find out, they won't like it—royal decree supersedes anything you do here."

"Then we try our damnedest to make sure they don't find out, and that we're ready for them when they do." She drummed her fingers on the document.

"You know you're talking treason."

"There's no reason for any of you to stay with me on this, might be safer to split up and hide out, take to the woods or something." She stared down at her hand, laid flat against the creamy smoothness of the king's parchment.

"No matter what they think, Jo, we're not animals, and we shouldn't have to live like that." He rested his arm on the tabletop, his huge, hairy hand not far from her own. "They told me what you brought them away from—even Koresh."

Joenna drew back. "Don't," she said. "Please, don't praise

me, Val. By the Lady, if you saw them—there's so many injured, and just plain worn-out from the war, and they get no rest, never mind the honor that should be due." Her fist beat the tabletop. "It's not enough. How could anything I do ever be enough?"

Valanor crept his hand across the table, and laid it alongside hers. "We do this the same way we did Joseph's Charge—one demon at a time, until we learn to do it better."

Silent, she nodded, waiting for the ache in her throat to subside.

He cracked a smile. "Hey—I've got tea, if you want, and even a kettle. Maybe it's a good thing I spent so long in the kitchen."

"Do y'know how many of you went off to war?"

Frowning. "Hard to say. There weren't quite two hundred at the training when we started out. That's all of us, assuming the army did their job."

Joenna studied his big, ugly face, those kettle-black eyes that held such depth. "The gate-soldier told me they were expecting less than sixty. Sixty left out of two hundred." She let it sink in, turning her hand in his as it tightened with his gasp. "The accursed king wants you dead, Valanor, and I'm not letting it happen."

"But what can we do?"

"If I could, I'd squat in that valley for weeks and bring 'em out one by one, but the army'll catch on to that, if they haven't already. Besides, I don't think there is a mine—I think the king's got something else on his mind and I don't like the smell of it. Gods, what I'd give for even one more full-blood on my side."

"Sick of us already, eh, Sergeant?" Koresh inquired, looming over them.

Valanor slid his hand away, and Joenna raised her fist, considering whether she should just have it out with the bastard right now. "If you're going to eavesdrop, Koresh, then make yourself comfortable—I've nothing to hide from you." Not quite true, but nothing interesting anyhow. "I need full-blood allies is to provide the cover for us to free every man in that camp, and wherever else they might be—if I had two more soldiers, and two more letters, we might have sprung dozens between the three of us." She shook her head, relaxing the fist. "Naw, that'll only work for so long, and I don't think we've got that much time."

"So what is the plan?" Koresh demanded, his harsh voice dropping from that height like a stone. "What madness have you thought up this time?"

Shane growled, "Leave it go, Koresh—have you forgotten already that we're only free on the sergeant's risk?"

Grunting with the exertion, Joenna climbed up on the table, avoiding the documents, and addressing herself to the room at large—from a height where she could see their faces. "Listen up. If we're going to free the rest of the scouts, we have to work together. What I've got in mind will be risky at best, and likely do no good. At worst, we'll reveal ourselves and our place, and the lot of us, me included, will lose our heads. If you're not willing—"she glared at Koresh—"then get out now and save us the worry."

Several others aimed their eyes the same direction, and

Koresh, for the first time, shifted under the anger, ducking his head. "I want to see us free as much as any of you. I just—I don't know why he does." He stuck a sharp finger in Joenna's direction.

"It's a good question," Lassiter admitted, with a rolling shrug.

"Right," she sighed, glancing down at Valanor, the only one who knew.

His dark eyebrow rose a little, and he said, "We're not in the army now, and Loref is more than avenged."

"Aye, Loref."

"Loref? What's he got to do with it?" Callifrax demanded. "He was my best friend."

Joenna's eye rested on Callifrax, thoughtful and clever, and a helpless grin broke over her face. "Aye, I'm glad to hear it. He was my son."

"Your son? But you—"the wide mouth dropped open, and shut with a snap, and a half-smile of his own.

"You're a woman?" Koresh crowed. "I knew there was something wrong with you!"

As if he hadn't heard, Callifrax murmured, "He talked about you all the time—used to drive us wild with jealousy that he had a mother who cared if he lived or died."

"She lied to us, just like all the rest of the full-bloods," Koresh tried again. "And worse than that, she sold her own son; how's that for love, eh?"

Someone growled, but Joenna faced her accuser. "Aye," she said, "you're right. I lied. I lied my way into an army that wouldn't take me to avenge my son's death. I did right well, if I do say so myself. And as for signing that paper, I can't read even my own name, let alone the rest of it. Then I lied myself into a corner: all this—"her arms open wide to take in the room and all that lay beyond—"everything we have is because the king thinks I'm his loyal man. Turns out he's wrong on both counts." She gave a wicked grin, and Valanor chuckled.

After the wonderment died down, she continued, "What it means is that everything you've got depends on that lie, and if it leaves this room, then we're all dead, clear?"

"Wait," Shane said, "If Loref was your son, then we've got an ally." His pointed grin spread slowly to match her own. "He rode with a knight and his man on this crazy lead they had, and they found the dragon, right?"

"That's where he died," Joenna confirmed.

"That knight, the dragon-slayer, he's the viceroy in Goshan now—it's got the generals worried because the man's a little mad himself. I overheard 'em talking when they learned the news."

For the second time that day, Joenna's heart leapt; they had a chance! "We'll send a message, if he can be persuaded. See, that's what we need: information, we need to know what's going on out there, if your absence is noticed, if there's other half-orcs who didn't get rounded up, because they will be soon I'm sure of it. You're all scouts, you know how to get around without being seen." Then her dancing eyes fell upon Rogan, still hovering near Brion's sickbed, and she stilled herself. "First, we need some rest, see to those wounds and such. Next, I'll want those who can write to copy out that message, the one granting safe-passage and naming me—you'll each need a copy, though we pray you don't have to use them. Joram, can you study the seal and copy that?"

"You're talking treason," he murmured, and a few other heads nodded.

"Aye," she said, "And any time one of you gets uncomfortable, you talk to me, or you leave—all I ask is you don't reveal the rest of us, right?"

Joram met her gaze, then his eyes flicked down to the documents on the table, with their flattened seals of wax. Slowly, he nodded. "I can do it."

"Good. We'll also need more money for weapons and supplies, what we got is nearly gone already."

"Got?" Valanor frowned. "How did you get any at all?"

She tipped the hilt of her new sword, showing the hollow place, and his eyes flared. She shrugged. "I don't need jewels," she told him.

"Money?" he prompted.

"Right. First, we gather the chestnuts. There's a market town a half-day's ride off, I'll sell the nuts and have a listen. Also," Joenna hesitated, then decided to plunge right in. "I'd like us to sell wound-cleansing ointment."

"What?" Koresh yelped, then turned furious eyes toward Valanor, who glowered back.

"You knew that I spit on the sergeant, that's why I got the barrel."

"Aye, but we didn't think he—she—knew! You've just given them another way to exploit us!"

"I'd just found out who she was, I wasn't about to let her

suffer!"

"She was happy enough to let you suffer," Koresh shot back, and Valanor surged to his feet.

"You don't know a thing about it," Valanor snarled, drawing himself up to his full height—a few inches over Koresh.

The others edged backward, while Lassiter got hold of Koresh's arm, only to be shaken away. Koresh snatched out the knife Joenna's sapphire had bought him.

Her vision blurred in her fury, and Joenna seized the ax from her belt.

"Don't," cried Joram, but she had no intention of shedding blood. Instead, she spun a half-circle and slammed the axe into the nearest beam. The room shuddered with the force of the impact.

"Stop it, both of you!" Joenna shouted.

The two froze, Koresh shifting the knife in his grip as he eyed her.

"What the hell is the matter with you?" she barked into Koresh's face, and he started. "I know you've had a rotten life—we all have!"

The sneer turned down his lips, and Joenna said, "Aye, go ahead and tell me how much worse it's been for you—and I'll tell you what it's like to be raped by orcs and thrown out in the cold for something you couldn't prevent. No, you bastard, you've got no right to look down on me, and accuse me. If you've got a problem with me, you bring it here—don't take it out on Val. So tell me, by every god, what is your problem?"

Koresh's grip on the knife tightened, and he drew it up a little closer. Tensing, Valanor prepared for the blow, but Koresh's eyes did not leave Joenna's face.

He wet his lips, and gave a shiver. "No," he said hoarsely. "I can't." For a moment, he looked back at Valanor, then his knife clattered to the floor, and Koresh sprang away, pushing through the room to flee through the open door.

CHAPTER

TEN

Ties That Bind

IN THE WAKE OF KORESH'S departure, they all remained silent for a long while, eyes lowered, the knife spinning on the floor until it slowed to a stop.

Finally, Joenna swallowed, and nodded. "Anyone know? Any clues?"

They shook their heads, and Lassiter volunteered, "He's always been like that, angry, ever since the army came. A bunch of us grew up in the same town, and I never saw him before."

"Aye. Well." She swallowed again, and reached up to pry the ax free from the beam, and lower it to the table. "You all know who I am, you know what I'm about. I'm glad of your company, and your help, if you're willing to give it. Get some rest, maybe doing some hunting or fishing, if you're up to that." At the thought of the lake, she mustered another grin. "Take a bath, or something."

It broke the tension, and they started to move away.

"What about you, Jo?" asked Valanor softly.

"Me? I'm going to stake a claim on yon sunny hillside and take a long, long nap." She pressed her hands to her back, then slowly unfastened her breastplate and let it drop to the tabletop. Shaking out her sweat-stained shirt, she said, "Gods, but that feels good."

Chuckling, Valanor nodded. "Go on and rest." He stepped over to where Brion lay. "Rogan, I'll watch him— you go find those herbs, eh?"

Joenna's legs barely wanted to move, but she got herself through the door and strolled up the slope a little ways, to one of the more plentiful patches of grass. Dropping down, she yanked off her boots and the reeking short-hose beneath, wriggling her toes into the cool depths of the grass. For a little while, she gazed over her territory, hearing the sounds of shouting and splashing from the lakeside, catching a glimpse of Rogan moving through the trees: so serious, that one. Sitting alone at last, Joenna laughed at herself. Damned if she didn't think of each one as a child of hers, each with his own ideas and problems; it would get her in trouble, this new mothering she'd taken up. She only hoped not to drive them all mad with her worries. It brought her back around to the problem of Koresh. She did all she could to be kind to him, then to stand up to him, to prove herself against his will, but he only got angrier. Ah, well. He'd gone off, and she thought it unlikely they'd see him again, not outside of a prison, anyhow. Or a barrel.

At last, Joenna lay back on the grass, and shut her eyes. The sun warmed her face, and a stray daisy tickled her ear. If Loref could be here now. . .

She woke up as the afternoon became chilly, and the shadows of chestnut trees crept up her bare feet. Rolling to her side, she saw a pair of legs, long, crossed, and she bolted upright, reaching for the ax that wasn't there. Her heart pounded in her ears, and she thought of Valanor sleeping outside of her tent, watching her back and missed him now.

With a breathy laugh, Koresh murmured, "I won't kill you."

Somehow, his uneven tone made the statement less comforting than it should have been.

"No," he continued, and she tried to make out his face against the brightness of the low sun, "if I decided to, I could've done it hours ago, before you woke."

"Not if it seemed important to look me in the eyes while you did it," she muttered in response, keeping still on her knees.

"Aye," he mused, "there is that." His large hands lay in his lap, fingering a scar on his ankle where no hair grew.

"You've been watching me sleep."

A nod.

"Why?"

A shrug, then he raised his head again, and let out a long breath. "You're good with secrets," he said. "You fight like a man, and just as well."

"Good of you to notice."

"Loref's mother."

She caught the subtle gleam of his eyes upon her, and she nodded.

"How could you stand the sight of your son? Didn't the sight of him make you think of what happened?"

Joenna relaxed a little, beginning to believe that he really wouldn't kill her. "Once in a while, maybe." She took a deep breath of her own, and told him something no one else in the world—even Valanor—knew. "Twice I put him in the cradle and walked away, into the woods. I thought, if I leave him behind, it'll all be undone. The second time, I got all the way to the road, and I imagined that I heard him crying. I turned right back around and ran home, in case he needed me. Never happened again after that."

The shrouded eyes slid shut, and he nodded. "I'll tell you—"his voice cracked—"I'll tell you, but you can't," he gasped a breath, his body trembling.

"Nobody hears it from me," she said softly. "Whatever you say, it stays with me."

The dark shadow that was Koresh stilled, though an outbreak of shivers rocked his body once in a while as he spoke. "They made me their slave, made me do the things they didn't want to—that's the only reason they kept me alive."

"Who?" she whispered.

"My mother had five children—her husband left her, after," one hand indicated the past, and Joenna understood. "She fed me her anger through her teats. When I was weaned, they put me to live in the shed with the pigs. When I got old enough to run away, they set the dogs to track me down and chained me after that." His fingers traced that mark around his ankle. "In the outhouse. If I cried, they shoved my head into the pit." His voice strengthened as he spoke through gritted teeth. "I fought back." His teeth glinted then, briefly. "You knew I would. They got a new chain, like a collar, sometimes so tight I couldn't speak. Sometimes—"his breath caught.

Joenna sat like stone, waiting and listening, desperate to maintain the balance that kept him talking.

"I dug the trenches and carried the fence posts and slaughtered the animals. If I moved too slow, they beat me. Sometimes, they beat me if I moved too fast. Sometimes they did it for spite. I got so angry, I just. . . I went mad. I got hold of one of the brothers. I would have ripped his throat out, but they got me off." A silent laugh that sent chills down Joenna's back. "I thought sure they'd kill me, and I would be free."

For a moment, he looked straight at her, the eyes glinting with shards of fire. "Everything the orcs did to you," he said, his voice like the edge of a blade that whispered from its sheath, "full-bloods did to me. Everything. It was weeks before I could walk again."

Joenna bit down on her outcry until he turned away, then pressed her hands to her mouth as a shaft of recollection shot through her. She longed for the words to comfort him, but the ancient pain still burned them both. For a time, they sat silent in the growing dusk. His hair gleamed almost brown like burnished leather.

"They heard the army was buying half-orcs and dragged

me down there for the money, and to be rid of me. Two of the boys were married, and the ones left over had gotten tired of the sport. The army did so much better by me that I never tried to run." Again, he laughed, and the sound of it struck Joenna through the heart so that she wished she could take him in her arms. "Oh, aye, I got the barrel a few times—I'm not much for authority, but you know that already." The laughter turned to hiccups and giggles.

Her muscles protested the long stillness, and Joenna knew that Koresh had no more to say. Clasping her hands together behind her head, Joenna stirred, stretching her aching back.

"You asked me to tell you," he said. "Did you like the story? Not a good one for campfires, but you might do something with it, if you could find a hero in it."

Carefully, Joenna replied, "I liked the bit where you got your hands at your brother's throat."

"Aye," he said, with a snort of laughter. "That's my favorite part."

"I'm still hoping that you win in the end."

"Not bloody likely—I'm bent for tragedy if anyone ever was. Naw, if you want a winner, then you look to Valanor. He's the kind that makes it through."

As if summoned by his name, Valanor's voice echo up the slope. "Joenna? Where are you?"

She rose, waving her arm, and Koresh sprang to his feet, crouching with his fists before him.

"Jo! Who's—Blue Lady! Are you alright? He's not hurt you." He bounded up the hill, his broken wrist slapping against his chest, and Joenna took a few steps forward to meet him, patting down his distress with both hands.

Valanor stopped, a spasm of pain crossing his face. "What's he doing here?"

"He's coming back," said Joenna firmly.

"What? You've got to see that he's dangerous, Jo, I know you want—"

"Hey!" she barked, and Valanor shut his mouth. She glanced up the slope at Koresh's face, lit now by the afternoon sun. He resumed his characteristic sneer, but his eyes shone with other things, and he lifted his chin at her look. Now that she knew, she caught the flash of a pale band that marked his throat, despite the dirt and sweat, still standing out from his skin. "If he wants to," she said slowly, "he's coming back."

Darting a glance to Valanor and back, Koresh murmured, "If you'll have me."

"Aye," she said, "we will."

"Joenna, you've got to see reason," Valanor protested. "We can't have him exploding like that every minute."

"If you're that set against him," she said, "you have the same choice as everyone else to stay or go."

He stiffened, and she instantly knew that she'd said it all wrong.

"No, Val, listen—"

"You'd chose him over me."

"Valanor, please—"

"I'll find another bowl for supper," he snarled, and pounded off down the hill.

"Sure you want me? I'm ruining things already." That

sharp edge returning to Koresh's voice.

Drawing an enormous breath, Joenna bellowed, "Someday!" Down the slope, Valanor hesitated, one foot still in the air. "Someday, the two of you are going to look each other in the eye, and tell your own godsdamned stories!"

A tall, dark statue Valanor stood, and slowly his head lowered, then he set down his foot and ran on.

"You."

Koresh crossed his arms. "Aye?"

"Come in for supper."

At that, his lips flinched toward a smile. "Naw, not yet." The smile fled, but the solemnity that replaced it warmed Joenna to her very core. "But I'll be there."

Her steps felt light as she moved down, boots in hand, bare feet reveling in the alternating scorched dry earth, then the soft wetness of the grass. She nearly bounced as she got down, then slowed coming through the trees. From inside came a chorus of loud, rough voices, talking and laughing, and the clatter of ladles and bowls. Spoons, she thought, adding that to the list of things they'd need to make—to make them large enough for half-orc hands. For a moment, memory cast her back to her own home, when she'd been very small. Three brothers and two sisters, her parents and grandfather gathered around the family table, barely big enough to fit them, but it didn't matter.

"A family," she whispered, naming the thing she so longed for through the lonely years, through the yet lonelier months since Loref's death.

Suddenly, a half-orc leapt through the door, knocking

his head, cursing and leaning against the wall to recover his balance. "Of all the stupid, brainless. . . " he muttered.

"Rogan?" Joenna pounced forward again, suddenly a sergeant. "What is it? Not Brion."

"Aye, Brion," he said behind his hands, then he let them fall and his eyes sparkled. "The fever's broken, Sergeant! He'll be alright."

"Good work!" She clasped his hand, and cocked her head again at the lintel, high above her own stature, then down to the threshold. "Tomorrow, we'll dig it out, deep enough for one of you."

"Aye, sir—that's an order I can live with."

CHAPTER
ELEVEN

Scout's Honor

THE NEXT FEW DAYS, ORDERS began in earnest. While Callifrax and Dale copied out letters of passage—and Valanor grumbled about the fact that he couldn't write with his wrist broken—the others worked on the manor and town, rounding up anything useful that Valanor might have missed. Brion, over his fever, sat for as long as he was able beside the piles, sorting out food and wine, needles, knives, and tools. Joram used a few of these latter to start work on forging a royal seal, testing it in candle wax until no flaw revealed it as different from the original. At last, he handed it over, and Joenna weighed it in her palm, the small weight of a thing which could be the end of all of them.

"Here we go, lads, after this, there's no turning back."

Koresh snatched up the stick of sealing wax and held it to

the flame, dropping an even spatter onto the first parchment. "I'm ready; are you?"

With a single nod, she pressed it down, and lifted the parchment to admire their handiwork. Holding it out to Koresh, she said, "Will you take daRives?"

The question stilled him, then he answered, "Aye. If you let me kidnap the Minister and drag him back in his own chains."

A few hoots of approval echoed around the room, and Joenna sighed. "It's a good thought, but no—that's about like killing the general to get out of the war: war goes on, and you've got twice the trouble."

His eyes narrowed. "You guessed it was me, that day."

"Who else? There's none other like you, Koresh."

"Praise be to the Gods," murmured Dale, and Valanor snorted with laughter.

The hint of a smile faded from Koresh's face, and Joenna stiffened for a fight, but he merely bobbed his head. "Aye, daRives."

"Keep in mind, we want information, we want to find your kin—we don't want to be rescuing your sorry hides, right?"

The scouts chuckled.

Valanor stirred and said, "Koresh. There's a garden by the eastern wing of the daRives manor, between there and the town." He took a deep breath. "It's been given over to the servants. They like to gossip in there, plenty of places to hide."

Joenna smiled. "So. I expect you back in four days, five

at the outside." She dripped the sealing wax and stamped another page. "Who's next?"

Koresh drifted back through the room, took up the small pack prepared for him, and paused a moment by the door. He caught her eye, and gave a slight bow, then vanished into the sun.

Shane stepped up, taking his paper, and his commission to travel as far as Goshan and sound out the viceroy, a journey of almost a week.

Lassiter and Callifrax, too, went out in opposite directions, learning the lay of the land and listening for their kin among the villages of the border.

Rogan, Joram, Dale and Brion—when he was up to it— she set onto making bows long enough for their own use, tending the livestock, finding herbs and stocking the larder with as much as they could lay in.

At last, with the others gone and Brion snoring on his pallet, Joenna faced Valanor who sat on the edge of a table, head bowed, hand curled in his lap. "I'm so bloody useless with this arm," he murmured.

She nearly laughed. "Useless? You got out a good spread at dinner last night, not to mention cleaning up this place."

"I'm not cut out to be a housemaid."

Softly, Joenna said, "I know, and I would not ask it of you."

"Then what? What's left for a one-armed man?"

"Just what you've always been good at—watching my back."

He gave a snort, but his head tilted a little to the side,

listening.

"We need you to fulfill our royal charter." She tapped the document on the table beside him. "Says here we need to keep a watch in that tower, and so we shall. You're the best of them, Val, even Koresh will admit to that—"a mistake, she saw in his sudden tension, but nothing for it now—"we need someone who'll know every inch of that view, every scent on that breeze, and every sound that comes up from the lake. Whatever's coming to find us, we need to know it before it can even be seen."

"Damn," he said to his lap.

"What?"

"You're right." Without looking at her, he rose and brushed past.

"Val, talk to me."

"I just did—and my sergeant gave me an order." He strode the length of the room and ducked under the low door, jerking it closed behind him.

The room felt suddenly cold with the wind of his passing, and Joenna shut her eyes against the ache of it. She couldn't reveal what Koresh had told her and why she should trust him, and Valanor wouldn't let her try. Every angle of his lean body showed his pain, and she had no idea what to do about it. At last, heaving a sigh, she rose and set about her own task: loading up the oxcart with bushels of collected chestnuts. From the piles Brion had sorted, she plucked a few garments, once so familiar, and transformed herself back into a woman. The rub of her legs irritated her under the long skirt, and she stared down at her breasts beneath the chemise. At last, she laughed as she thought how nice it would be to get comfortable again at the end of the day, in the men's garb she had become used to. For now, though, she wrapped a kerchief around her head, covering her ragged hair, and hoped she could play the part.

"Jo?" croaked a soft voice behind her, and she turned to find Brion watching from beneath heavy eyelids. "Going to market?"

"Aye, I'm off—back tomorrow."

"Wait." He wriggled his hands under his pillow, and revealed them again with a trio of small bottles, tightly corked. "The demon-ointment you wanted."

Approaching, she squatted down—completely unfeminine—and brushed the hair back from his eyes. "I thought you all weren't up for that."

One of his shoulders moved beneath the blanket. "Some are, some aren't. Those who are've been spitting in bottles all night." He took a few breaths, and continued, "Some still hate the full-bloods. Why should we help the ones who hurt us, eh?" His lips twitched into a smile. "And some of us think we're better than that."

Taking the bottles, she told him, "Aye, you are. Thanks." Rising again, trying not to stumble over her skirts, she took her leave, and clambered up into the cart, the precious bottles resting beside her. She made her way up the slope and back down the road to the town at the crossroads, the meeting of the ways lined on both sides with carts and tents full of peasants hawking all manner of goods. Nudging her ox down the line, Joenna pushed her way between a jeweler and knife-maker: both merchants likely to attract the trade of a returning soldier. After staking the ox in back, she spread a blanket in her little space and put out the baskets of nuts. Whenever a likely subject approached, she cried her wares, offering the ointment at a penny a rub, or a pound for a bottle—money returned if it didn't work.

The first taker, a scruffy old soldier with a nasty limp narrowed his eyes at her. "Money back?"

"Aye, sir, if it don't work."

"How'll you be sure if it does?"

Shrugging, she offered a grin, knowing her features were unlikely to inspire confidence. "I guess I'll have to trust you, sir."

"Mmm." He dug out a grubby purse, and selected a single penny which he dropped into her palm, then dragged up the leg of his pants to reveal a festering wound. "Gashed me good with one o'them swords."

The mention of it made her shoulder throb, and she nodded. "Oh, aye, those're wicked blades to be sure."

"You saw some fighting, did you?"

Joenna kept her head ducked as she spilled a splash of ointment onto her hand and started to spread it over the wound. Someone—Rogan, she guessed—had dressed it up with a few sweet-scented herbs. "My son was in it. This here's his idea." Well, it was near enough the truth that it wouldn't trip her up.

"Aye, well, all it's done for me is sting," the man snarled, reaching down to grab the penny from her fist.

She half-rose to take it back, when he stopped, still bent,

and his mouth dropped open. "I'll be, it works!" The penny slipped back from his grasp, and Joenna caught it, dropping it into a purse of her own.

"Thank you kindly, sir. Tell your mates!"

Wondering eyes turned on her, and he said, "I'll do that."

By noon the next day, her stock had sold out, and she was sworn to return two days later with more—lots more. A spring in her step, Joenna walked along the line and perused the wares of the other merchants. She'd heard little of use, aside from a rumor that someone would come to re-claim the village of Glamshire. Finding what she was after, Joenna waited for a space to open in the press of bodies around a metal-smith's portable workshop. She edged in among the men and fingered the arrowheads—some triangular, some diamond-shaped, a few with four sides and just a bit of flare.

"Here," she called, holding one up. "How much for these?"

"Those? You don't want those, they're for armor, left over from the war. What's your prey? Rabbits? Deer?"

Damn this woman's garb, she thought, then framed her story. "My son's to be the sheriff at Glamshire—you heard? So, we need to be ready if the orcs come calling, eh?"

The big man chuckled. "Ain't been no orcs calling in near twenty years, ma'am. We pushed 'em clear back to the next river."

"Still," she said, setting her jaw in that stubborn way, "King's charter says to be ready, so ready we'll be—and won't you thank us for it if the enemy comes."

His broad shoulders rose and fell. "Suit yourself. How

many?"

"Twelve dozen, for a start."

"Tw--?" He propped a hand on his hip. "Maybe you should send your son down to discuss it."

"And hasn't he got better things to do than to haggle with you?" She freed her now-plump purse and dropped it onto the table before her with a satisfying clink of coins.

"Very well, I'll have them for you—"

"In two days," she cut in.

He furrowed his brow at her, and finally nodded. "Two days, a pound in advance."

Joenna counted out the coins, leaving her purse nearly empty, and handed them over. "Thank you, sir, and my son thanks you." She pushed her way back out again, leaving a murmur among those behind her.

She'd not gone five paces before she felt a stealthy hand at her purse. With a quick movement, she snatched the waiting ax—in case she needed firewood, naturally—and hacked a deep gouge into the arm.

The young man screamed, clutching the wound, and staggered off before the merchants could get hold of him.

"Smartly done," observed the metal smith.

With a nod of thanks, Joenna wiped the ax at the hem of her skirt and slipped it back into its loop, then resumed her stroll, humming a song she swore she had forgotten years ago. She bought a few geese and whetstones, loaded these into the cart, and headed for home, spirits still high and a few coins yet to jingle in her hidden purse. Whoops, hollers and laughter drifted up from the area of the lakeside as Joenna crested the hill then dropped down to lead the cart the last part of the distance to the tumble-down barn behind the manor. When she came around the corner, geese in tow, Valanor burst from the door and nearly knocked her down.

"Did you see them?" he demanded, breathless, looking far beyond her.

"Naw. Who'm I looking for? We're not expecting anyone for three more days."

Dale appeared from the edge of the woods, carrying an armload of straight, slender saplings, bobbing his head to Joenna as he came up. "Well, so you are a woman after all," he observed, standing his bundle up against the wall.

Ignoring him, Valanor paced a little ways up the road, then back, and Joenna caught the hint of a flush in his cheeks. "There's three half-orcs on the way, from the south— they must be keeping to the woods around the lakeside, but I caught wind of them."

"Aye, well, that's good, then." Joenna dragged a hand across her brow, hoping for a drink and maybe a dip in the lake before supper.

"Have a look at these, Sergeant," Dale began. "Are they—"

"You don't understand!" Valanor leaned to see her over the stand of saplings. "They're women, too." Meeting her gaze for the first time since Koresh's departure, his black eyes gleamed against the new color in his complexion.

Joenna stifled a giggle, but Dale let fly with his own laughter. "Yes, well, if all babies were boys, there wouldn't be no more, would there?"

At that, Valanor growled, and Joenna pointed out, "He grew up alone, so did Loref, for that matter—never met their own kind until the army."

"Sorry, Val." Dale turned, giving his full attention to straightening the saplings, sorting them by some mysterious method.

"For a minute there," Valanor muttered, "I thought Koresh had come back early, and his sharp tongue with him."

Dale said, "I am sorry, right? I just, the mention of women. . . " Then he faced them, and his forehead furrowed. "I'm married."

"Married? But that's not allowed, is it?" Joenna asked.

He spread his hands. "Nor is this, but we do it anyhow. Nobody knows—I've been afraid to send for her." His hands fell back to dangle against his legs. "If this works, we'll finally have a place we can live as man and wife."

Suddenly both half-orcs froze, sniffing as the breeze shifted, and Valanor grinned. "They're almost here."

Joenna hid her smile in a yawn, and said, "Well, I'll go and transform myself—the fewer know the truth—for now—the better." She followed the new descent into the manor and found her battle-weary clothes, gratefully changing from woman back into man, keeping only the ax as her constant companion.

By the evening of the eighth day, their number had grown from ten to twenty-two, all half-orc women discovered by the scouts on their separate missions. The young women—plumper than their male counterparts, but no less tall—had lived secret lives tending fields and sheep for their families.

They whispered that their number was fewer because a stunned family might rationalize another son as a help to its unwilling parents, but a girl, even such a big one, could hardly be expected to be of much use since she couldn't marry. Lassiter loped in just after dawn, and Callifrax appeared in the afternoon, drifting in like smoke from the fields. Shane would be out for more than a week yet, assuming he made it as far as Goshan and the viceroy who might support their cause.

After bathing, the returned scouts settled in the midst of the growing company and relayed their news. Their captured kin up north had been set to cleaning up the battlefields— burning the demons and burying the men who had not been claimed by their lords or families.

"And," Lassiter concluded, taking another swig from a jug Brion had discovered, "our people are burned with the demons, scouts along with the enemy."

A rumble of disgust filled the big room, and Joenna said, "Blue Lady, it must be awful for them—all that rot, not to mention just the stink of the demons themselves."

Heads bobbed their agreement. "It's a good way to save money on feeding them if they can't keep a meal down," Valanor said.

"Any word from Koresh?" Lassiter asked, passing on the jug.

Nobody answered, and Joenna shifted on her table. "It's only just time, he'll be in during the night, I expect."

Perhaps it was that thought that woke her early, but Joenna couldn't sleep again, despite the snoring of those who slept around her in the loft. She rose and picked her way among them, down the stairs to the main hall. A few more dark forms littered the floor here, and she scanned them for a moment by the dim light from the glowing embers, and that pale edge of dawn reaching through the tall windows. Koresh still had not arrived. Finding a blanket to ward off the morning's chill, Joenna stepped through the small door into the tower where most of the women lay, curled together to keep warm. She mounted the ladder in the corner, taking her up to the next floor and the one above that, finally emerging through a trapdoor onto the top level of the tower.

"How goes the night?" she murmured.

The still shape of Valanor stirred, turning his face from the distant light of dawn. "Nearly over, now." He regarded her for a moment as she drew nearer, then he said, "He's not back yet."

"Tell me you've not stayed up all night waiting for him," she sighed, as if she hadn't.

"Naw, just took over from Joram. Does it matter, though? The point is, he's not coming back."

"I don't believe that."

He smote the wall with a strong left fist. "Why not? Why can't you accept the facts? We'll just be lucky if he's not turned us over to the Minister."

"He wouldn't—he hates full-bloods."

"Yourself included," said Valanor darkly.

Crossing her arms, tugging the blanket closer about her shoulders, Joenna replied, "Maybe so, but I don't think he'd betray us. I chose him for daRives because he'll never be broken."

"You're the most stubborn woman in the world, you know that? Great Gods, Joenna, see reason! Koresh does whatever he pleases, and whatever will most anger somebody else. He'd do it just to foul you up—"

"Val, you don't know him—"she broke off, regaining her balance. "You only know what he wants you to. You've not had much call to trust anyone in your life, but I'm asking you to trust me: Koresh has every reason to be angry, but he would never betray his own, even if they've thrown their lot in with a full-blood."

Towering above her, his face unseeable, Valanor made a low sound at the back of his throat that brought a shiver to Joenna's spine. His head bowed for a moment, his good hand rubbing the elbow of the broken arm, then he sank down before her and looked up into her face. "I know you want to see the best in everyone, Jo," he murmured. "I'd hardly be here myself if you hadn't believed in me, but there are some people who are beyond your power to reach."

"Every one of us has good in him, Val, even the ones who look most foul."

His eyes fell, and he laughed lightly, his breath puffing mist into the growing day. "By the same token, Joenna, you've got to see that everyone has evil, too. Look at my family," he said, then, more softly, "Or look at yours."

"Maybe he's decided not to come back, he's taken himself into hiding."

"Maybe," Valanor agreed, "but we can't afford to believe that. We have to act as if they already know what we're up to.

We have to act as if the army is already on the march."

Joenna shut her eyes, digging her knuckles into them. "Damn."

Warm, calloused fingers brushed against her cheek, and she tilted her head a little, resting her face against Valanor's enormous palm. "You're right," she whispered.

"Of course I'm right. These plans of yours, Joseph Lorefsdam, it's time to put them into action."

"Aye," she said, and reluctantly raised her head. "I'm getting too old for this."

"So you keep telling me, but I've yet to see you lie down and rest."

"Soon," she sighed into the dawn, and feared it might be all too soon as the chill breeze found its way to her flesh and she shivered.

Together, they watched the sun rise, then descended the ladders to set the battle-plans in motion.

CHAPTER

TWELVE

A Man of Worth

"WE'VE GOT BOWS ENOUGH FOR half of you," Joenna told the assembled half-orcs after breakfast. "Anyone experienced?" A few nodded shaggy heads. "Good—train a few more, use our own arrows for practice and save the new ones for when they're needed. The rest of you are on construction, except whoever's helping Joram make swords."

The handy thing about Glamshire, as Joenna had observed on their first day over the hill, was that it lay in this little valley, hemmed in by the lake and mountains and a dense band of trees. The only clear approach for an army— one without boats, anyhow—was over that very same hill, hence the stone wall that stood over her head, and the ruins of a watch-tower taken down by the dragon. This, they pulled apart to re-enforce the wall, then they diverted the stream that bubbled down along the path until it flowed over and built themselves a bridge. All the while, they heard the swish and plunk of arrows from the archery drills. Joenna stumped up and down the hill all day long it seemed, checking on this, and answering questions about that—supervising the various projects, helping the agile Rogan to pick out good trees. They worked steadily all that day, and most of the next—ten days, she thought, and perhaps Shane had reached Goshan, and was even now securing the viceroy's assistance. In eight or nine more days, they might have all the allies they needed.

A shrill whistle—learned from Joenna herself—echoed across the valley, and the workers froze. A few arrows flew wild.

Brion glanced down from the area of the bridge, his dark eyes meeting hers, and Joenna remembered to breathe. "It's just war," she muttered. "Just another bloody war." She turned and ran for the tower, gripping the ax that hung by her side.

Valanor met her at the door. "It's daRives," he said, his face grim. "Hard to say how many, but at least a hundred mounted—"he hesitated, then added, "There's three half-orcs in the party."

"Koresh?"

A single nod.

Her chin dropped to her chest. "Damn it! I wish—" she broke off, forcing back her emotions.

"I know," he said. "Me, too."

"Anything else we should know?"

He shrugged. "A scent of blood. I'll know more when they come into view. We've got two hours, maybe less."

"I'll go kill the horses," she said, and he grimaced as he turned away.

Joenna hurried her company into order with mumbled best-wishes and whatever encouragement her busy mind could come up with, which wasn't much. At Valanor's second whistle, she climbed the ladders and stared down with him at the on-coming army—just a small one, she knew from her months of service, but enough to take them down and have some to spare. The banners of daRives fluttered from spear-tips, and the Minister himself rode before them. Close behind him came the three half-orcs, and even she could identify Koresh's paler hair among the horsemen, though she caught only glimpses of his down-turned face. The other two wore collars of iron that glinted dull in the sun and turned her stomach.

As the company drew near, the horses balked, rearing and backing, and several riders lost balance and fell. Joenna wanted to laugh, for they did look ridiculous trying to control the frightened animals, but the blood from her own two horses still rimmed her ax just as it splashed the walls and bridge up on that hill. They needed any advantage, and would make any sacrifice.

"It's not too late to run," she remarked.

Valanor shook his head. "It was too late the moment we realized we might be free."

"But if we all die here, what's the use? We can't do the rest any good by dying."

"We've talked it all out, Jo," he said gently. "We're through with dying for other people's glory. Have you forgotten

Joseph's Charge? We'd still rather die on the field than to live as slaves."

Nodding slowly, she drew out her sword of knighthood and offered it to him, hilt-first.

Valanor narrowed his eyes at it. "That's the sword the king gave you."

"Aye, well, yours is too big to swing with one hand—I've seen you trying it. This'll be a bit short, but quick, too."

He laughed. "Like you."

"Aye, like me, and don't you forget that, soldier."

"Aye, sergeant." He lifted the sword from her grasp and aimed it toward the approaching enemy. "Then it must be time."

A smaller party of men dismounted, letting the majority retreat, and crossed over the bridge, the half-orcs included. From here, the lurch of Koresh's limp looked more pronounced. None of their own company was in sight. They were as ready as they could be.

"Aye," she said, "It's time."

Joenna and Valanor emerged from the trees, side by side, and waited in the field at the bottom of the hill while the Minister and his men advanced, a white banner unfurled over their heads.

"Greetings, Minister," Joenna called out. "What's your flag for?"

DaRives drew nearer, his handsome face looking pale and sharp as he eyed the pair of them. "And a good day to you, Joseph. The flag is a mere precaution. Did you not invite me to sup with you when you'd gotten settled?"

Joenna flicked a glance toward Koresh—she couldn't help herself—but he did not look up. "So I did, but I didn't expect to be feeding so many." She spread her hands and smiled, but it felt forced. "Sorry about your horses. I guess they don't like my bridge."

With a gracious nod, Gracyn daRives accepted the apology. As he lifted his head, his eyes lingered on the sword that hung by Valanor's side, and his lips pinched together. Joenna stiffened, expecting accusations. Instead, daRives inquired, eyebrow raised, "What happened to your sword, Joseph? Your gemstone's gone missing."

"Oh, aye. Thieves I expect."

"Yes, well, you do chose untrustworthy company." His silvered head inclined slightly in the direction of Koresh.

Was there blood on the scout's lips? The other two half-orcs, in their chains, hunched together, jaws clenched. "Dunno about that, sir," said Joenna slowly. "I've yet to find them wanting."

Among the soldiers of the enemy, Koresh flinched, but she caught the flash of his eyes under that shag of hair.

"Them?" said daRives, examining his fingernails. "I wasn't aware you had more than one."

Blue Lady, Joenna wailed inside her head, unsure if it was a curse or a prayer. This game was too much for her, and he knew it. Setting her feet a little wider apart, Joenna shrugged. "They come and go, I guess. They know where they're welcome."

"Maybe so, Joseph, but you know they were to be sent for re-training. If you are harboring fugitives from that order, it would be wise to turn them over, rather than to risk the king's displeasure."

"Fugitives, sir?" She exchanged a glance with Valanor, mainly to be sure he was still with her. "Not that I know of."

At that pronouncement, daRives expelled a long breath and folded his arms. "We know what's going on here, Joseph," he said, almost gently. "It will be best for you to confess yourself. I can intervene on your behalf, perhaps we might claim that your war-wounds caused a temporary leave of your senses."

The lovely voice drifted like a song upon the wind, but that single word—we— stung her, as if she and the Minister belonged on the same earth, never mind in the same sentence together, ugly, stubby Joenna, mother to orcs, and Gracyn daRives, the disdainful and elegant lord at the king's right hand. "I don't believe I have, sir, but it's kind of you to inquire."

"My dogs found that—"a sharp gesture toward Koresh— "in my garden a few days ago, and it has a very interesting story."

At her side, Valanor gave an almost inaudible growl. "I told him about that garden," he muttered.

Across the short space between them, Koresh shook his head, but it sagged lower.

"You see," daRives continued, his pleasant demeanor beginning to crack, "we thought they'd all gone for re-training, aside from the one we gifted to you. In doing a little. . . research, we found that a few were missing from their camp, including this one. It seems a soldier showed up on, so he said, the king's orders. We spoke to several guards there, and found that a soldier of remarkably similar appearance returned on several occasions." He held out one gloved hand, and made a show of counting on his fingers. "Eight times, to be precise, each time leaving with one of the scouts formerly under your command. Shall I go on?"

"Feel free. They're saying I stole a few half-orcs and did what with them?"

"Don't play the fool with me! I don't know what's come over you—you, a decorated Knight of the Realm—that you insist on this betrayal of the king's own trust. Is it worth your lands, and quite possibly your life?"

She looked him in the eye, feeling the intensity of the silence all around them.

Gracyn daRives stared back, his face like iron.

Quietly, simply, she said, "Yes."

CHAPTER

THIRTEEN

One More Demon

WITH A LOOK OF UTTER amazement, daRives asked, "Why? Is it not enough that they lie to you and steal from you? That they carry your secrets into the wrong hands?" He flipped out a piece of parchment that fluttered to the ground: Koresh's forged document. "And you think we don't know what you're up to? The women who've disappeared from the fields, the renegades hiding out here. Great Gods, Joseph, you're not that stupid."

"He knows," Valanor whispered. "Do it now."

In the haze of anger, the heat of betrayal that filtered through her, Joenna clenched her fists. "Aye, sir, maybe if you let me put some questions to your informant, we can get it hammered out, eh?"

DaRives flicked his hand, and two of his men escorted

Koresh out from their ranks and propelled him across the grass. He staggered a few steps, and dropped to his hands and knees, trembling violently.

"You're welcome to him," said the Minister, and his skin looked a shade more gray in the full light, "but you'll find my men have already dealt with him as traitors should be dealt with."

A cold fear clutched at Joenna's guts, but she took a few steps forward. A trail of blood marked Koresh's crooked path to where he had fallen, his too-small feet no longer supporting him. The sight slapped away her voice and will, and she stood a moment gawking: they had cut off his toes. Someone had cauterized the wounds, but walking had reopened them. The swollen puncture marks of bites showed against his arms, leading up to the torn skin that overlaid the earlier scars at his wrists. Blood streamed, too, from his lips as he wept without sound, and she realized what daRives meant, that Koresh had lost his sharp tongue for good this time. Maybe he had supped on rage as an infant. Maybe he hated her, and maybe telling her his secrets had been the latest of his humiliations before the full-bloods, but how could he betray his kin? Even under torture. She had expected him to die first.

Joenna's vision seemed black. Koresh crumpled there before her was the weakest, most pathetic thing she had ever seen. She hefted her ax and strode forward, drawing a few cheers from the Minister's company as she stood over Koresh. He put up a hand—missing two fingers—to protect his neck, then let it fall as if it no longer mattered. Why couldn't he have run away? Why couldn't he have just died?

"Jo, you thought he'd never break," Valanor murmured, but Joenna shot him a look and he said no more, his own eyes revealing that mix of fear and sadness that gripped her. Their battle was already done, before they had a chance to fight.

Jo, she thought, and fury blasted through her despair.

Dropping to one knee beside her man, she gathered his head to her chest, her fingers wrapped through his deep-brown hair. "You're still with us, Koresh. You're home."

His tears burned through the thin fabric of her sleeve as he leaned into her, his battered arm clinging to hers, and she cursed the breastplate that put any distance between them.

Grimly, the ax in her hand, Joenna lifted her eyes to the Minister's. "What have you done?"

Gracyn daRives swallowed. "What would you have me do? He said—"

"He told you nothing," she roared as Valanor came up beside her.

"Sergeant, I—"

"Val," she cut him off, bracing herself against the convulsive shaking of Koresh's tortured body. "He told them nothing, Valanor." Distinctly, she said, "They still don't know who they're dealing with."

"Jo, I don't—" He broke off in a moan of comprehension and dropped down to the grass, laying his hand on Koresh's back. "I'm sorry, Koresh, by all the Gods of Heaven and Earth—" His face crumpled in shame.

"Get him to Rogan, I'll keep 'em talking a little longer."

Joenna muttered over the fallen man.

Valanor gave a sharp nod and gathered Koresh over his shoulder with his good arm as Joenna surged to her feet.

"You, sir, are despicable!" She had meant to say something more diplomatic, but the black fury clouded her mind and vision and the ax yearned for blood.

"Joseph, really—"

"They made us track him," blurted one of the half-orc prisoners. "Everywhere he'd gone, they said he was a killer, they said—"

A knife appeared in a soldier's hand and hacked across the prisoner's throat so that his final words came out in a gush of blood. Stepping back, they let him fall.

Joenna's own throat felt dry, as coarse as a demon's skin, and the wild eyes of the second scout caught hers. Shifting her grip, Joenna raised the ax, first to her chest, then, in a sudden movement, swung it over her head and howled as she plunged into the Minister's guard.

The bridge over the stream groaned with its ropes and pulleys, and slammed up into place, cutting off the main part of daRives's force. Arrows whistled from the chestnut trees, and men screamed.

Joenna paid no heed to the execution of her plans. Instead, she dove among the threshing legs and found a pair clad in ragged gray, the huge feet unshod and dirty. She barreled into them, grabbing the scout and dragging him down.

The half-orc cried out as he fell, and she pulled herself alongside, keeping him down. Blood streamed from cuts on his neck and face, and she knew she had gotten him just in time. Overhead, a flustered would-be assassin shouted for help and got none.

Joenna gripped the scout's shoulder, meeting the flash of the dark eyes. "You're okay. When I tell you, you run—get out toward the mountains if you can. If we're still here by nightfall, we'll do your chains—if not, best of luck to you."

Bleeding and frightened he managed to stammer, "Thank you, Sergeant."

Giving a sharp nod, Joenna rose to one knee, warding off the frantic soldiers around her. Then she sprang to her feet, hacking left and right, and a pathway broke before her. "Go, go, go!"

The scout scrambled up and ran, and she lost sight of him as the men milled before her. Some of them ran as well, toward the wall that had sealed itself before them, while others clustered around their leader.

One soldier still gripped his bloody knife, stumbling over the body of the dead scout in his panic.

Hefting the ax, Joenna hesitated. Though she had killed before, her arms resisted the swing. She had never before struck her own kind. DaRives's words flashed through her: was it worth her lands, her life, to fight her own people for these half-breeds?

Joenna ducked a wild slash of the knife and slipped on the blood-stained grass. Before her flushed face, the dead scout lay on his side, in chains, unable to ward off the blade that killed him.

Yes! the word shot through her with a savage intensity.

Yes, she would kill, yes she would die, yes would give anything to see these people freed, not just for her son's sake, but for their own. Yes!

Bellowing, Joenna swung her ax. It slammed the man's arm and the knife flew. He was fumbling with his sword when she struck him down.

The Minister's smaller troop fled for the sheltering trees—or they would have been shelter, if not for her half-orc company hiding among them. Bows turned, enormous arrows ripped through the soldiers.

The survivors ran for the manor-house, and Joenna cursed. Valanor needed time to get Koresh to the healer—even if it was the last thing any of them ever did. Leaving the road and the fight behind her, she sprinted down a narrow path and came to the house just as the Minister and his men burst from the trees.

Brilliant blue eyes sparked at her and daRives shouted, "We'll rout you from your holes like the vermin you are! My men will crash through that wall and rip this place to ruins!"

"My archers are on that wall," she snarled back, and his momentum broke, his sword drawn, but put up as he mastered his breathing, looking wary.

"They fired on men under the flag of parlay." He slowed, each pace now deliberate as his men formed up around him.

"You cut the throat of an innocent man," she answered, "the kinsman of my company, in spirit if not in flesh. After you tortured one of our own."

"They are beasts, not men, Joseph. Get it through your skull—their fathers came to rape and kill—it's all they're good for!"

"You know nothing!" she shot back. "Rogan's a healer, his mother taught him. Joram worked that seal as well as any full-blood." As daRives advanced, Joenna slowly retreated, circling until she stood with her back to the door.

DaRives swept the forest with a gesture. "What are they doing now but killing?"

"For their lives, and their freedom," she said. "Because you taught them to, because you made them believe their lives weren't even worth dying for." Her breathing thundered in her ears with the drumbeat of her heart as the Minister came on, treading carefully, as if he faced a wild boar. His features worked their magic, convincing her that he heard, that he was listening, even through his anger.

DaRives's lips parted, his brow furrowed, and he slowly shook his head. "I thought I was getting through to you, that day in court," he murmured, the shadow of grief returning. "You speak so lightly of sacrifice, Joseph, but you don't know. If you had seen how my wife suffered for this punishment she had not brought upon herself."

Wetting her lips, Joenna said, "I have seen it."

Across the slight distance, the Minister stared.

"I have seen it in her own son's face," she told him.

Someone moved up behind her, filling the doorway, and Gracyn daRives's piercing gaze flared a little wider. "Hallo, Sergeant, what did I miss?" Valanor asked, his voice a deep river of emotion that rolled over her head.

"Nothing," the Minister answered. "You're just in time for the end."

Up the hill, something gave a terrible crash, and hoof beats pounded over the fallen gate. Men cheered as they came.

Leather swished as Valanor drew his blade. "Don't worry, Jo," he murmured. "I've got your back."

For perhaps the last time, Joenna raised her ax. She stuck two bloody fingers in her mouth and whistled. High above, her archers drew and loosed their long shafts. Two men fell, clawing at the arrows that took them.

Trapped between the archers in the woods, and those on the tower, the soldiers scattered. Half-orc swordsmen rose up to meet them. They could kill all this lot, Joenna realized, every man in the clearing, but the arrows would not last forever, then the horsemen would be upon them, and would show them no mercy. Her own plan sickened her, for she could see nothing but death.

Then the thought swept by her, for daRives and five others sprang forward, using the bulk of the building to defend them.

From their sheltered doorway, they could be attacked by two men at most, and Joenna's ax bit deep into a leg while Valanor's borrowed sword skewered an arm, then a throat.

To one side, something broke and crashed. Joenna risked a glance and caught sight of a pair of boots as their wearer plunged through the shuttered window.

"Val, behind you!"

Even as she shouted, another man grabbed the sill and heaved himself through the opening.

Valanor spun away, and Joenna disarmed the new

combatant, then caught the unhinged door with the edge of her ax and flung it sideways over the entrance. Stumbling backwards, she tipped the mass of broken furniture they had carefully arranged and the room went suddenly dark as tables blocked out both swords and sun.

In the dim light, she slammed her back to the wall. Three men danced by before her—two soldiers, and Valanor, fighting left-handed, his teeth gritted. But where--?

As she framed the question, she felt the blow, a stabbing pain that lanced her arm. Jerking it tight to her body, she rolled along the wall, her weight ripping the sword from its bearer's hand. It clattered away as she took the offensive, facing off against the Minister of War, the leader of the king's knights and legendary warrior.

Her stomach clenched as he drew a long dagger.

A wave of pain wracked her arm, and her left shoulder ached in sympathy. Behind her, Rogan shouted, bounding down the stairs to their aid.

Raising up the ax, she dodged DaRives's first swipe, only to be caught with a backhand blow from a table-leg she hadn't seen him take. Too old for this, she thought dully.

Still, she dropped and turned, slicing up toward his belly, forcing daRives to leap and flounder into a table. Driving forward, she swung again.

The ax carved flesh. The Minister cried out and whirled away his wounded leg, landing another blow with the stick.

As he shot forward, dagger in hand, Joenna blocked him, grunting at the effort. This time, she swept the ax back again immediately, before his off-hand weapon caught her.

The ax-blade bit into wood and was wrenched upward as the knife swung down. It skittered across her breastplate and slashed across her underarm.

Joenna shrieked as the ax handle slid from her nerveless grasp and she thudded to the floor. Instinctively, she slapped her shoulder, letting out a puff of gratitude as she discovered her arm was still there.

DaRives threw aside his stick, his two hands wrapping the handle of her own ax.

About to become a notch, Joenna lay paralyzed, numb with the pain.

"Joenna!" someone screamed, a sound that echoed through her vacant mind.

A huge shadow came between herself and the blade, with a ringing clang. Valanor stumbled, his sword caught against the table, and a second blow shattered the blade, but the ax lodged in the tabletop, the two men face to face over Joenna's cowering form. The ax jerked free. Valanor's hand stretched, searching a weapon.

Snatching the charter, Valanor gave it a snap, unfurling the scroll in the Minister's face.

Cursing, daRives staggered back, ripping it away. He barely had time to swing the ax as Valanor came at him again.

Barely, but it was enough. The familiar ax cut through the air, its silvered edge slipping from light into shadow again.

A howl tore from her as she lifted herself to her knees. Valanor stepped back, tripping, falling sideways.

With an awful thud the flat of the ax slammed into his head.

The blow spun him around and sent him crashing to the floor.

"No! No," her voice broke into a wail. Her arm rose of its own accord to block the next swing, her eyes unable to focus on anything but Valanor's sprawled body.

Overhead, a wrenching sound drew the attacker's attention. A section of the ceiling ripped away and someone leapt through, smacking daRives with the broken board. Together, they tumbled, knocking Joenna back to the floor.

She rolled and hearthstones scraped down her back. Her outflung hand found something strong and hard, and slick with blood. She felt the notches under her groping fingers and rose, her ax in hand.

Before the fireplace, daRives lay on the floor, tearing at his opponent, a much larger man who produced a moan to shiver the dead. Koresh got hold of the Minister's shoulders and rapped his head against the floor. The struggling hands went still.

Joenna looked down at the ax in her hands. Black hairs clung in the blood that oozed along the blade. With a cry, she cast it into the fire and staggered forward.

A leg tripped her, sending her to her knees. She tried to crawl, the patch of sunlight before her broken by a figure plunging through the window. "My lord!" someone shouted.

Scuffling broke out, and someone whimpered.

Before her, beyond the light, Valanor lay still, his broken arm under him, his face hidden by that black unruly hair. Joenna crawled.

A hand descended from the sky and seized her, hauling

her up. It shook her like a puppy. "Don't kill him," daRives ordered, his voice booming into her face, "not yet."

"You've won," she croaked, dangling from his grip, her left arm hanging at a strange angle. "Let me go to him."

"Shut your mouth, Sergeant," said a soldier's voice, "or we'll kill the lot!"

Joenna's head flopped sideways, her strength ebbing away. In the corner, she saw Koresh, held with a blade across his throat. The pale mark of his slavery shivered with each raspy breath. Black eyes like twin cauldrons blinked at her through the gloom. They shifted to the side, then back, and the bloody lips curled up into a sneer.

With a sudden twist, Koresh broke the grip and clamped his jaws around the man's arm.

The Minister looked back at his scream. Joenna's fingers pried free her buckles and she shook herself, sliding sideways, her shirt torn open. One sleeve and the dangling breastplate hung from the Minister's grasp.

Joenna struck the floor and rolled. She got her feet under her, propelling herself the last few steps until she fell beside him. "Valanor? Oh, Val, don't be dead, please don't be dead."

Crouching over him, she stroked the hair from his face, the sticky warmth of blood coating her fingers. She crept her fingers down the line of his jaw, feeling for a pulse she could not find. Pressing closer, she shook away the tears that clouded her eyes. Not now, not yet.

"Holy Father and Mother, you're a woman," breathed Gracyn daRives.

"Of course I'm a bloody woman, what does it matter?"

she cried. "You stole my first son and murdered him, now you've taken Valanor, too."

Floorboards creaked as the Minister approached. "I don't understand. You fought in the army," he said slowly, "you lead that charge. For your son, am I right? Or was that also a lie?"

"No lie." Her head jerked up and she glared. "I fought for the sake of the son you stole!" She jabbed a finger at him as if she could strike him dead. "His father was an orc, a monster, but Loref was mine. He was all I had in the world to love and your bloody soldiers wouldn't even tell me where he fell!" Gently, she rolled Valanor to his back, taking his head upon her lap, his blood soaking through her trousers.

DaRives limped a little nearer, his eyes ranging from her ravaged face to her revealed breast, finally settling back on her face, with a trace of a smile. "Lorefsdam. Your little jest. But if you went through. . . what happened to you, how could you stand to even look at them? "

"Only half of them is orc," she said, letting her hand drop down to Valanor's chest, "the other half is up to us. You treat Val like he's a beast, and you forget that half of him is hers, and always has been. He used to sit outside the servants' door, listening to you reading her stories and wishing he could be like one of those heroes, sent down by the gods to save her life. He didn't know what he had done wrong, but he would have done anything to make it right."

"How could he make it right?" DaRives demanded. "He wasn't even there!"

The words echoed around the chamber. The injured men

groaned and stirred, Rogan cradling an injury of his own. Koresh, in his corner, pounded his fist on the floor, drawing another whimper from the man he held.

At the center, Gracyn daRives did nothing, said nothing. Slowly, Joenna raised her eyes. "If she had known her son, my lord, would she be here now, defending him?"

The man towered regally over her, his hands hanging limp at his sides while his mouth formed words with no voice. His face turned down, and, for the first time, he studied the wounded man she cradled in her lap. His head tilted a little to one side and he squinted down at Valanor's face, then his eyes widened as if he noticed something he hadn't seen before. His lips moved, forming the name of a woman long dead.

The chest beneath Joenna's hand shuddered and rose with a gasping breath, then another. Never taking her eyes from the Minister, Joenna felt a grin split the dumb mask of her face.

"Jo. . ." a whisper.

"Aye, Val, I'm here."

"How many?" he breathed.

"How many?" she echoed, and looked down into his black eyes.

"Notches, for the ax."

Gripping his hand, she said, "We just slew our last demon."

If you enjoyed Joenna's Ax, look for the first Tale of
Bladesend, *Winning the Gallows Field*

In spite of Trelayne's victories in battle, the road home
is longer than the young knight ever imagined, and it must
begin with rejecting his peasant companion, Derik, and
denying the memory of the half-orc companion who gave
his life for them. Forced to admit that the battle has changed
him, Trelayne tries to be the champion for the peasantry,
only to make things worse—Derik imprisoned, his betrothed
rejecting him, his war-wounds throbbing. Honor provokes
him to claim a duel with the swordmaster in the hopes of
earning Derik's freedom, but the veterans find that winning a
battle is not the same as winning a war—and not all demons
wear an ugly face.

Elaine Isaak, writing as E. C. Ambrose, is also the author
ofThe Dark Apostle series, from DAW books : magic,
intrigue, medieval surgery

Elisha Barber, July, 2013
England in the fourteenth century: a land of poverty and
opulence, prayer and plague, witchcraft and necromancy.
Where the medieval barber-surgeon Elisha seeks redemption
as a medic on the front lines of an unjust war, and is drawn
into the perilous world of sorcery by a beautiful young witch.

In the crucible of combat, at the mercy of his capricious superiors, Elisha must attempt to unravel conspiracies both magical and mundane, as well as come to terms with his own disturbing new abilities. But the only things more dangerous than the questions he's asking are the answers he may reveal...

Elisha's adventures continue in an additional 4 volumes.
Traditional fantasy novels by the same author:

The Singer's Crown
Available in a variety of ebook formats from Rocinante

When his uncle murders his family to take the throne, Prince Kattanan DuRhys is the only royal left alive. . . at a terrible cost. Stripped of his manhood, Kattanan travels as a court singer from one wealthy patron to the next. Given as a courtship gift to the young Princess Melisande, Kattanan feels the stirring of emotions he thought were denied him. But her jealous fiancée has other plans--and the sinister magic to carry them out.

Must Kattanan sacrifice his song to win his kingdom, and the woman he loves?

The Eunuch's Heir
Available in a variety of e-book formats, from Rocinante

Prince Wolfram of Lochalyn can't possibly live up to the reputation of his father, the Blessed Rhys, so why bother to try? Until a series of self-started catastrophes plunges him into the midst of the growing refugee population. They claim to be fleeing a war, and only Wolfram sees the danger that lurks in their mysterious ways. But his love for an exotic stranger, and his concern for the princess who pursues him collide with a more terrible struggle, in which his kingdom may fall and his very Goddess be brought to Her knees. Discredited by his past and disdained by his own mother, Wolfram must find the truth of his birth, and fight to make amends for all that he's done—or be seduced by the darkness of distant power.

The Bastard Queen
Available in a variety of e-book formats, from Rocinante

Beloved bastard of an unloved king, Fiona will do almost anything to please her father, even studying magic though she never shows more than a spark of talent. But the plague that grips their city sends her to work with the dying, as enmity builds between the two peoples her father has brought together. When arson burns a hospital, everyone blames the growing racial tension, until an unexpected suspect comes from the woods on a spirit-quest destined to uncover the secrets of Fiona's past. Then Reynaud, long Fiona's suitor, suddenly asks to marry her sister. Struggling to find a cure for the plague, Fiona becomes ever more convinced that its emergence is no coincidence—and that Reynaud may be leading a conspiracy that will end in genocide.

About the Author

Elaine Isaak is the author of *The Singer's Crown* (Eos, 2005), and its sequels, as well as the "Tales of Bladesend" epic novellas comprising *Joenna's Ax* in full-length, and *Winning the Gallows Field*. As E. C. Ambrose, she writes "The Dark Apostle" historical fantasy novels about medieval surgery, which began with *Elisha Barber* (DAW 2013), and continue with *Elisha Magus* (2014), *Elisha Rex* (2015), *Elisha Mancer* (2017), and concluding with *Elisha Daemon* (2018). Her short fiction has won the Tenebris Press Flash Fiction contest and appeared in the New Hampshire Pulp Fiction series, *Fireside* magazine and *Uncle John's Bathroom Reader*. A graduate of the Odyssey Speculative Fiction workshop, she has returned to teach there as well. In addition to writing and teaching about writing, Elaine works part time as an adventure guide and rock climbing instructor. Visit www.TheDarkApostle.com or www.ElaineIsaak.com to find out why you do not want to be her hero.

facebook.com/ElaineIsaak
or twitter @elaineisaak